Richard Doddridge Blackmore

Alice Lorraine

A Tale of the South Downs

Richard Doddridge Blackmore

Alice Lorraine
A Tale of the South Downs

ISBN/EAN: 9783744678100

Printed in Europe, USA, Canada, Australia, Japan

Cover: Foto ©Andreas Hilbeck / pixelio.de

More available books at **www.hansebooks.com**

ALICE LORRAINE.

A TALE OF THE SOUTH DOWNS.

BY

RICHARD DODDRIDGE BLACKMORE,

AUTHOR OF "THE MAID OF SKER," "LORNA DOONE," ETC.

ὅντως ἔχει σοι ταῦτα, καὶ δείξεις τάχα,
ἔιτ' εὐγενὴς πέφυκας, ἔιτ' ἐσθλῶν κακή.
SOPH. *Ant.*

IN THREE VOLUMES.
VOL. I.

LONDON:

SAMPSON LOW, MARSTON, LOW, & SEARLE,

CROWN BUILDINGS, 188, FLEET STREET.

1875.

CONTENTS OF VOL. I.

ALICE LORRAINE.

CHAPTER I.

ALL IN THE DOWNS.

WESTWARD of that old town Steyning, and near Washington and Wiston, the lover of an English landscape may find much to dwell upon. The best way to enjoy it is to follow the path along the meadows, underneath the inland rampart of the Sussex hills. Here is pasture rich enough for the daintiest sheep to dream upon; tones of varied green in stripes (by order of the farmer), trees as for a portrait grouped, with the folding hills behind, and light and shadow making love in play to one another. Also, in the breaks of meadow and the footpath bendings, stiles where love is made in earnest, at the proper time of year, with the dark-browed hills imposing everlasting constancy.

VOL. I.

Here no man, however lame he may be from the road of life, after sitting awhile and gazing, can help feeling that he is refreshed and even comforted. Though he hold no commune with the heights so far above him, neither with the trees that stand in quiet audience soothingly, nor even with the flowers still as bright as in his childhood, yet to himself he must say something—better said in silence. Into his mind, and heart, and soul, without any painful knowledge, or the noisy trouble of thinking, pure content with his native land and its claim on his love are entering. The power of the earth is round him with its lavish gifts of life,— bounty from the lap of beauty, and that cultivated glory which no other land has earned.

Instead of panting to rush abroad and be lost among jagged obstacles, rather let one stay within a very easy reach of home, and spare an hour to saunter gently down this meadow path. Here in a broad bold gap of hedge, with bushes inclined to heal the breach, and mallow-leaves hiding the scar of chalk, here is a stile of no high pretence, and comfortable to gaze from. For hath it not a preface of planks, constructed with deep anatomical knowledge, and delicate study of maiden decorum? And lo! in spite

of the planks—as if to show what human nature
is—in the body of the stile itself, towards the
end of the third bar down, are two considerable
nicks, where the short-legged children from the
village have a sad habit of coming to think.
Here, with their fingers in their mouths, they
sit and think, and scrape their heels, and stare
at one another, broadly taking estimate of life.
Then with a push and scream, the scramble and
the rush down-hill begin, ending (as all troubles
should) in a trackless waste of laughter.

However, it might be too much to say that
the cleverest child beneath the hills, or even
the man with the licence to sell tea, coffee, snuff,
and tobacco, who now comes looking after them,
finds any conscious pleasure, or feels quickening
influence from the scene. To them it is but a
spread of meadows under a long curve of hill,
green and mixed with trees down here, brown
and spotted with furze up there; to the children
a play-ground; to their father a farm, desirable
at so much per acre.

So it is : and yet with even those who think
no more of it, the place, if not the scenery, has
its aftermath of influence. In later times, when
sickness, absence, or the loss of sight debars
them, men will feel a deep impression of a

thing to long for. To be longed for with a yearning stronger than mere admiration, or any limner's taste can form. For he, whatever pleasure rises at the beauty of the scene, loses it by thinking of it; even as the joy of all things dies in the enjoying.

But to those who there were born (and never thought about it), in the days of age or ailment, or of better fortune even in a brighter climate, how at the sound of an ancient name, or glimpse of faint resemblance, or even on some turn of thought untraced and unaccountable, again the hills and valleys spread, to aged memory more true than ever to youthful eyesight; again the trees are rustling in the wind as they used to rustle; again the sheep climb up the brown turf in their snowy zigzag. A thousand winks of childhood widen into one clear dream of age.

CHAPTER II.

"How came that old house up there?" is generally the first question put by a Londoner to his Southdown friend leading him through the lowland path. "It must have a noble view; but what a position, and what an aspect!"

"The house has been there long enough to get used to it," is his host's reply; "and it is not built, as they are where you live, of the substance of a hat."

That large old-fashioned house, which looks as if it had been much larger, stands just beneath the crest of a long-backed hill in a deep embrasure. Although it stands so high, and sees much less of the sun than the polestar, it is not quite so weather-beaten as a stranger would suppose. It has some little protection, and a definite outline for its grounds, because it was

built on an old and extensive settlement of the
chalk; a thing unheeded in early times, but now
very popular and attractive, under the name of
"landslip."   Of these there are a good many
still to be traced on the sides of the Sussex
hills, caused (as the learned say) by the shifting
of the greensand, or silt, which generally under-
lies the more stable chalk.   Few, however, of
them are so strongly marked and bold as this
one, which is known as " Coombe Lorraine."   It
it no mere depression or irregular subsidence,
but a perpendicular fall, which shows as if a
broad slice had been cut out from the chine to
the base of the highland.

Here, in the time of William Rufus, Roland
de Lorraine, having a grant from him, or from
the Conqueror, and trusting the soil to slide no
more, or ignorant that it had ever slidden, built
himself a dwelling-place to keep a look-out on
his property.   This abode, no doubt, was fitted
for warlike domesticity, being founded in the
fine old times when every gentleman was bound
to build himself a castle.

It may have been that a little jealousy of his
friend, De Braose (who had taken a larger
grant of land, although he was of newer race,
and had killed fewer men than Sir Roland), led

this enterprising founder to set up his tower so high. At any rate, he settled his Penates so commandingly, that if Bramber Castle had been in sight, he might have looked down its chimneys as freely as into his villeins' sheepcotes. Bramber Castle, however, happened to be round the corner.

This good knight's end, according to the tradition of the family, was not so thoroughly peaceful as a life of war should earn. One gentle autumnal evening, Sir Roland and his friend and neighbour, William de Braose, were riding home to a quiet supper, both in excellent temper and spirits, and pleasant contempt of the country. The harvest-moon was rising over breadths of corn in grant to them, and sheep and cattle tended by their villeins, once the owners. Each congratulated the other upon tranquil seizin, and the goodwill of the neighbourhood ; when suddenly their way was stopped by a score of heavy Englishmen.

These, in their clumsy manner, sued no favour, nor even justice ; only to be trodden down with fairness and show of reason. .
: "Ye shall be trodden all alike," De Braose shouted fiercely, having learned a good deal of English from the place he lived in ; " clods are

made to be trodden down. Out of my road, or I draw my sword!"

The men turned from him to Sir Roland, who was known to be kind of heart.

"Ye do the wrong thing to meet me thus," he answered in his utmost English; "the thing, that is to say, I hearken; but not with this violence."

Speaking thus he spurred his horse, and the best of the men made way for him. But one of them had an arrow straining on the cord, with intent to shoot—as he said to the priest at the gallows—De Braose, and him only. As the two knights galloped off, he let his arrow, in the waning of the light, fly after them; and it was so strongly sped that it pierced back-harness, and passed through the reins of Roland de Lorraine. Thus he died; and his descendants like to tell the story.

It is not true, although maintained by descendants of De Braose, that he was the man who was shot, and the knight who ran away Sir Roland. The pious duties rendered by the five brave monks from Fécamp were for the soul of Sir Roland, as surely as the arrow was for the body of De Braose. But after eight hundred years almost, let the benefit go between them.

Whichever way this may have chanced, in an age of unsettled principles, sure it is that the good knight died, either then or afterwards. Also, that a man was hanged at a spot still shown in his behalf, and that he felt it such an outrage on his sense of justice, after missing his proper shot, that even now he is often seen, when the harvest-moon is lonely, straining a long bow at something, but most careful not to shoot.

These, however, are mere legends, wherewith we have nought to do. And it would have been as well to leave them in their quiet slumber, if it could have been shown without them how the house was built up there. Also one may fairly fancy that a sweet and gallant knight may have found his own vague pleasure in a fine and ample view. Regarding which matter we are perhaps a little too hard on our ancestors; presuming that they never owned such eyes as ours for "scenery," because they knew the large impossibility of describing it.

CHAPTER III.

LINEAGE AND LINEAMENTS.

WHETHER his fathers felt, or failed to see, the beauty beneath their eyes, the owner of this house and land, at the time we have to speak of, deserved and had the true respect of all who dwelled below him.

It is often said that no direct descendant, bred from sire to son, still exists (or at any rate can show that he has right to exist) from any knight, or even cook, known to have come with the Conqueror. The question is one of delicacy, and therefore of deep feeling. But it must be owned, in candour, upon almost every side, that there are people, here and there, able to show something. The present Sir Roland Lorraine could show as much in this behalf as any other man in England. Here was the name, and here the place; and here that more fugitive being, man, still belonging to both of them.

Whether could be shown or not the strict red line of lineage, Sir Roland Lorraine was the very last man likely to assert it. He had his own opinions on that all-important subject, and his own little touches of feeling when the matter came into bearing. His pride was of so large a nature, that he seldom could be proud. He had his pleasant vein of humour about almost everything, wholly free from scoffing, and most sensitive of its limit. Also, although he laid no claim to any extensive learning, or especially accurate scholarship, his reading had been various; and his knowledge of the classics had not been allowed to fade away into misty memory.

Inasmuch as he added to these resources the further recommendation of a fine appearance and gentle manners, good position and fair estates, it may be supposed that Sir Roland was in strong demand among his neighbours for all social purposes. He, however, through no petty feeling or small exclusiveness, but from his own taste and likings, kept himself more and more at home, and in quietude, as he grew older. So that ere he turned sixty years, the owner of Coombe Lorraine had ceased to appear at any county gatherings, or even at

the hospitable meetings of the neighbourhood.

His dinner-party consisted only of himself
and his daughter Alice.   His wife had been
dead for many years.   His mother, Lady Valeria, was still alive and very active, and having
just numbered fourscore years, had attained the
right of her own way.   By right or wrong, she
had always contrived to enjoy that special
easement ; and even now, though she lived
apart, little could be done without her in the
household management.

Hilary, Sir Roland's only son, was now
at the Temple, eating his way to the bar, or
feeding for some other mischief ; and Alice, the
only daughter living, was the baronet's favourite
companion, and his darling.

Now, whether from purity of descent, or
special mode of selection, or from living so long
on a hill with northern consequences, or from
some other cause, to be extracted by philoso-
phers from bestial analogies—anyhow, one thing
is certain, these Lorraines were not, and had
not for a long time been at all like the rest of
the world around them.   It was not pride of
race that made them unambitious, and well
content, and difficult to get at.   Neither was it

any other ill affection to mankind. They liked
a good man, when they saw him ; and naturally
so much the more, as it became harder to find
him. Also they were very kind to all the poor
people around them, and kept well in with the
Church, and did whatever else is comely. But
long before Sir Roland's time all Sussex knew,
and was content to know, that, as a general rule,
"those Lorraines went nowhere."

Neighbours who were conscious of what we
must now begin to call "co-operative origin"
felt that though themselves could claim justices
of the peace, high sheriffs, and knights of the
shire among their kin, yet they could not quite
leap over that romantic bar of ages which is so
deterrent, perhaps because it is so shadowy.
Neither did they greatly care to press their
company upon people so different from themselves, and so unlikely to admire them. But
if any one asked where lay the root of the
difference, which so long had marked the old
family on the hill, perhaps no one (least of all
any of the Lorraines themselves) could have
given the proper answer. Plenty of other folk
there were who held aloof from public life.
Simplicity, kindness, and chivalry might be
found, by a man with an active horse, in other

places also : even a feeling, as nearly akin as
our nature admits to contempt of money, at that
time went on somewhere. How, then, differed
these Lorraines from other people of equal rank
and like habits with them ?

Men who differ from their fellows seem, by
some law of nature, to resent and disclaim the
difference. Those who are proud, and glory in
their variance from the common type, seldom
vary much from it. So that in the year of
grace 1811, the mighty comet that scared the
world, spreading its tail over good and bad,
overhung no house less conscious of anything
under its roof peculiar, than the house of
Coombe Lorraine.

With these Lorraines there had been a
tradition (ripened, as traditions ripen, into a
small religion), that a certain sequence of
Christian names must be observed, whenever
allowed by Providence, in the heritage. These
names in right order were Roland, Hilary, and
Roger ; and the family had long believed, and
so had all their tenants, that a certain sequence
of character, and the events which depend upon
character, might be expected to coincide with
the succession of these names. The Rolands
were always kindly proud, fond of home and of

their own people, lovers of a quiet life, and rather
deep than hot of heart. A Hilary, the next of
race, was prone to the opposite extremes, though
still of the same root-fibre. Sir Hilary was
always showy, affable, and romantic, eager to do
something great, pleased to give pleasure to
everybody, and leaving his children to count
the cost. After him there ought to arise a
Roger, the saviour of the race ; beginning to
count pence in his cradle, and growing a yard
in common-sense for every inch of his stature,
frowning at every idea that was not either of
land or money, and weighing himself and his
bride, and most of his principles, by troy-
weight.

CHAPTER IV.

FATHER AND FAVOURITE.

Upon a very important day (as it proved to be, in his little world), the 18th of June, 1811, Sir Roland Lorraine had enjoyed his dinner with his daughter Alice. In those days men were not content to feed in the fashion of owls, or wild ducks, who have lain abed all day. In winter or summer, at Coombe Lorraine, the dinner-bell rang at half-past four, for people to dress; and again at five, for all to be down in the drawing-room. And all were sure to be prompt enough; for the air of the Southdown hills is hungry; and Nature knew what the demand would be, before she supplied her best mutton there.

When the worthy old butler was gone at last, and the long dark room lay silent, Alice ran up to her father's side, to wish him, over a sip of wine, the good old wish that sits so lightly on the lips of children.

"Darling papa, I wish you many happy, happy returns of the day, and good health to enjoy them."

Sir Roland was sixty years old that day; and being of a cheerful, even, and pleasant, though shy temperament, he saw no reason why he should not have all the bliss invoked on him. The one great element in that happiness now was looking at him, undeniably present and determined to remain so.

His quick glance told that he felt all this; but he was not wont to show what he felt; and now he had no particular reason to feel more than usual. Nevertheless he did so feel, without knowing any reason, and turned his eyes away from hers, while he tried to answer lightly.

This would not do for his daughter Alice. She was now in that blush of time, when everything is observed by maidens, but everything is not hinted at. At least it used to be so then, and still is so in good places. Therefore Alice thought a little, before she began to talk again. The only trouble, to her knowledge, which her father had to deal with, was the unstable and romantic character of young Hilary. This he never discussed with her, nor even alluded to it; for that would have been a breach of the law in all duly-entailed conservatism, that the heir of the house, even though a fool, must have his folly kept sacred from the smiles of inferior members. Now, Hilary was ·not at all a fool ; only a young man of large mind.

Knowing that her father had not any bad news of Hilary, from whom he had received a very affectionate letter that morning, Alice was sorely puzzled, but scarcely ventured to ask questions; for in this savage island then, re-spect was shown and reverence felt by children towards their parents; and she, although such a petted child, was full of these fine sentiments. Also now in her seventeenth year, she knew that she had outgrown the playful freedoms of the babyhood, but was not yet established in the dignity of a maiden, much less the glory of womanhood. So that her sunny smile was fading into the shadow of a sigh, when instead of laying her pretty head on her father's shoulder, she brought the low chair and favourite cushion of the younger times, and thence looked up at him, hoping fondly once more to be folded back into the love of childhood.

Whatever Sir Roland's trouble was, it did not engross his thoughts so much as to make him neglect his favourite. He answered her wistful gaze with a smile, which she knew to be quite genuine; and then he patted her curly hair, in the old-fashioned way, and kissed her forehead.

"Lallie, you look so profoundly wise, I shall put you into caps after all, in spite of your sighs, and tears, and sobs. A head so mature in its wisdom must conform to the wisdom of the age."

"Papa, they are such hideous things! and you hate them as much as I do. And only the other day you said that even married people had no right to make such frights of themselves."

"Married people have a right to please one another only. A narrow view, perhaps, of justice; but—however, that is different. Alice, you never will attend when I try to teach you anything."

Sir Roland broke off lamely thus, because his child was attending, more than himself, to what he was talking of. Like other men, he was sometimes given to exceed his meaning; but with his daughter he was always very care-

ful of his words, because she had lost her
mother, and none could ever make up the
difference.

"Papa!" cried Alice, with that appealing
stress upon the paternity which only a pet child
can throw, "you are not at all like yourself
to-day."

"My dear, most people differ from themselves, with great advantage. But you will
never think that of me. Now let me know
your opinion as to all this matter, darling."

Her father softened off his ending suddenly
thus, because. he saw the young girl's eyes
begin to glisten, as if for tears, at his strange
new way.

"What matter, papa? The caps? Oh no;
the way you are now behaving. Very well then,
are you quite sure you can bear to hear all
you have done amiss?"

"No, my dear, I am not at all sure. But I
will try to endure your most heartrending
exaggerations."

"Then, dear papa, you shall have it all.
Only tell me when to stop. In the first place,
did you, or did you not, refuse to have Hilary
home for your birthday, much as you knew that
I wanted him? You confess that you did.

And your only reason was something you said about Trinity term, sadly incomprehensible. In the next place, when I wanted you to have a little change to-day, Uncle Struan for dinner, and Sir Remnant, and one or two others——"

"My dear, how could I eat all these? Think of your Uncle Struan's size."

"Papa, you are only trying now to provoke me, because you cannot answer. You know what I mean as well as I do, and perhaps a little better. What I mean is, one or two of the very oldest friends and relations to do what was nice, and help you to get on with your birthday; but you said, with unusual ferocity, 'Darling, I will have none but you!'"

"Upon my word, I believe I did! How wonderfully women—at least I mean how children—astonish one, by the way they touch the very tone of utterance, after one has forgotten it."

"I don't know what you mean, papa. And your reflection seems to be meant for yourself, as everything seems to be for at least a week, or I might say——"

"Come, Lallie, come now, have some moderation."

"Well, then, papa, for at least a fortnight.

I will let you off with that, though I know it is much too little. And when you have owned to that, papa, what good reason can you give for behaving so to me—me—me, as good a child as ever there was?"

"Can 'me, me, me,' after living through such a fortnight of mortification—the real length of the period being less than four hours, I believe—can she listen to a little story without any excitement?"

" Oh, papa, a story, a story! That will make up for everything. What a lovely pleasure! There is nothing I love half so much as listening to old stories. I seem to be living my old age over, before I come to any age. Papa, I will forgive you everything, if you tell me a story."

"Alice, you are a little too bad. I know what a very good girl you are; but still you ought to try to think. When you were only two years old, you looked as if you were always thinking."

"So I am now, papa; always thinking— how to please you, and do my best."

Sir Roland was beaten by this, because he knew the perfect truth of it. Alice already thought too much about everything she could

think of.   Her father knew how bad it is, when
the bright young time is clouded over with
unseasonable cares ; and often he had sore
misgivings, lest he might be keeping his pet
child too much alone.   But she only laughed
whenever he offered to find her new com-
panions, and said that her cousins at the rectory
were enough for her.

"If you please, papa," she now broke in
upon his thinking, "how long will it be before
you begin to tell me this beautiful story ? "

"My own darling, I forgot ; I was thinking
of you, and not of any trumpery stories.   But this
is the very day of all days to sift our little
mystery.   You have often heard, of course,
about our old astrologer."

"Of course I have, papa—of course !   And
with all my heart I love him.   Everything the
shepherds tell me shows how thoroughly good
he was."

"Very well, then, all my story is about him,
and his deeds."

"Oh, papa, then do try, for once in your
life, to be in a hurry.   I do love everything
about him ; and I have heard so many things."

"No doubt you have, my dear ; but perhaps
of a somewhat fabulous order.   His mind, or

his manners, or appearance, or at any rate
something seems to have left a lasting impression upon the simple folk hereabout."

"Better than a pot of money; an old woman
told me the other day it was better than a pot
of money for anybody to dream of him."

"It would do them more good, no doubt.
But I have not had a pinch of snuff to-day.
You have nearly broken me, Alice; but still
you do allow me one pinch, when I begin to tell
you a good story."

"Three, papa; you shall have three now,
and you may take them all at once, because you
never told such a story, as I feel sure it is
certain to be, in all the whole course of your life
before. Now come here, where the sun is
setting, so that I may watch the way you are
telling every word of it; and if I ask you any
questions you must nod your head, but never
presume to answer one of them, unless you are
sure that it will go on without interrupting the
story. Now, papa, no more delay."

CHAPTER V.

Two hundred years before the day when Alice thus sat listening, an ancestor of hers had been renowned in Anatolia. The most accomplished and most learned prince in all Lesser Asia was Agasicles Syennesis, descended from Mausolus (made immortal by his mausoleum), and from that celebrated king, Syennesis of Cilicia. There had been, after both these were dead, and much of their repute gone by, creditable and happy marriages in and out their descendants, at a little over and a little under, twenty-two centuries ago; and the best result and issue of all these was now embodied in Prince Agasicles.

The prince was not a patron only, but also an eager student of the more recondite arts and sciences then in cultivation. Especially he had given his mind to chemistry (including alchemy), mineralogy, and astrology. Devoting himself

to these fine subjects, and many others, he seems
to have neglected anthropology ; so that in his
fiftieth year he was but a lonesome bachelor.
Troubled at this time of life with many expos-
tulations—genuine on the part of his friends,
and emphatic on that of his relatives—he held a
long interview with the stars, and taking their
advice exactly as they gave and meant it,
married a wife the next afternoon, and (so far
as he could make out) the right one. This
turned out well. His wife went off on the
occasion of her first confinement, leaving him
with a daughter, born A.D. 1590, and all women
pronounced her beautiful.

The prince now spent his leisure time in
thought and calculation. He had almost made
his mind up that he was sure to have a son ; and
here was his wife gone ; and how could he risk
his life again so ? Upon the whole, he made up
his mind, that matters might have been worse,
although they ought to have been much better,
and that he must thank the stars, and not be
too hard upon any one; and so he fell to at his
science again, and studied almost everything.

In that ancient corner of the world, old Caria,
the fine original Leleges looked up to the prince,
and loved him warmly, and were ready by night

or day to serve him, or to rob him. They saw that now was the finest chance (while he was looking at the stars, with no wife to look out for him) for them to do their duty to their families by robbing him; and this they did with honest comfort, and a sense of going home in the proper way to go.

Prince Agasicles, growing older, felt these troubles more and more. As a general rule, a man growing older has a more extensive knowledge that he must be robbed of course; and yet he scarcely ever seems to reconcile himself with maturing wisdom to the process. And so it happened to this good prince; not that he cared so very much about little trifles that might attract the eye of taste and the hand of skill, but that he could not (even with the aid of all the stars) find anything too valuable to be stolen. Hence, as his daughter, Artemise, grew to the fulness of young beauty, he thought it wise to raise the most substantial barrier he could build betwixt her and the outer world.

There happened to be in that neighbourhood then an active supply of villains. Of this by no means singular fact the prince might well assure himself, by casting his eyes down from the stars to the narrow bosom of his mother

earth. But whether thus or otherwise fore-
warned of local mischief, the Carian prince took
a very strong measure, and even a sacrilegious
one. In or about the year of our reckoning,
1606, he walled off his daughter, and other
goods, in a certain peninsula of his own, clearly
displayed in our maps, and as clearly forbidden
to be either trenched or walled by a Pythia
skilled in trimeter tone, who seems to have
been a lady of exceptionally clear conservatism.

The prince, as the sage of the neighbourhood, knew all about this prohibition, and that
it was still in force, and must have acquired
twenty-fold power by the lapse of twenty
centuries; and as the sea had retreated a
little during that short period, it was evident
that Jove had been consistent in the matter.
" He never meant it for an island, else he
would have made it one." Agasicles therefore
felt some doubt about the piety of his proceed-
ing, retaining as he did, in common with his
neighbours, some respect for the classic gods.
His respect, however, for the stars was deeper,
and these told him that young Artemise was
likely to be run away with by some bold adven-
turer. A peninsula was the very thing to suit
his purpose, and none could be fairer or snugger

than this of his own, the very site of ancient
Cnidos, whereof Venus once was queen.

Undeterred by this local affection, or even the
warnings of Delphi, the learned prince exerted
himself, and by means of a tidy hedge of paliure
and aspalathus made the five stades of isthmus
proof against even thick-trousered gentlemen,
a fortiori against the natives all unendowed
with pantaloons.   Neither might his fence be
leaped by any of the roving horsemen—Turks,
Cilicians, Pamphylians, Karamanians, or reavers
from the chain of Taurus.

This being fixed to his satisfaction, with a
couple of sentries at the gate, and one at either
end, prompt with matchlocks, and above all, the
young lady inside provided with many proverbs,
Prince Agasicles set forth on a visit to an
Armenian sage, reputed to be as wise as himself almost.   With him he discussed Alhasen,
Vitellio, and their own contemporary, Kepler,
and spent so many hours aloft, that on his
return to his native place he discovered his own
little oversight.   This was so very simple that
it required at least a sage and great philosopher
to commit it.   The learned man appears to
have forgotten that the sea is navigable.   So it
chanced that a gay young Englishman, cruising

about in an armed speronera, among the Ægæan
islands, and now in the Carpathian sea, hunting
after pirates, heard of this Eastern Cynosure,
and her walled seclusion. This of course was
enough for him. Landing under the promon-
tory where the Cnidian Venus stood, he fell,
and falling dragged another, into the wild maze
of love.

Mazed they seemed of course, and nearly
mad no doubt to other folk. To themselves, however, they were in a new world altogether, far
above the level and the intellect of the common
world. Artemise forgot her pride, her proverbs,
and pretensions; she had lost her own way in
the regions of a higher life; and nothing to her
was the same as it had been but yesterday.
Heart and soul, and height and depth, she
trusted herself to the Englishman, and even left
her jewels.

Therefore they two launched their bark upon
the unknown waters; the damsel with her heart
in tempest of the filial duties shattered, and the
fatherland cast off, yet for the main part anchored
firmly on the gallant fluke of love; the youth in
a hurry to fight a giant, if it would elevate him
to her.

Artemise, with all her rashness, fared much

better than she deserved for leaving an adoring
father the wrong side of the quickset hedge.
The bold young mariner happened to be a
certain Hilary Lorraine, heir of that old house
or castle in the Southdown coombe. Possessed
with the adventurous spirit of his uncles, the
famous Shirley brothers, he had sailed with
Raleigh, and made havoc here and there, and
seen almost as much of the world as was good
for himself or it.

Enlarged by travel, he was enabled to sup-
press rude curiosity about the wishes of the
absent prince; and deferring to a better season
the pleasure of his acquaintance, he made all
sail with the daughter on board, as set forth
already; and those two were made into one,
according to the rites of the old Greek Church,
in the classic shades of Ida. And to their dying
day it never repented either of them—much.

When the prince returned, and found no
daughter left to meet him, he failed for a short
time to display that self-command upon which
he had for years been wont to plume himself.
But having improved his condition of mind by
a generous bastinado of servants, peasants, and
matchlock men, he found himself reasonably
remounting into the sphere of pure intellect.

In a night or two an interesting conjunction of heavenly bodies happened, and eclipsed this nebulous world of women.

In a few years' time he began to get presents, eatable, drinkable, and good. Gradually thus he showed his wisdom, by foregoing petty wrath ; and when he was summoned to meet a star, militant to his grandson, he could not help ordering his horse.

CHAPTER VI.

THE LEGEND CONTINUED.

ALTHOUGH this prince knew so much more of the heaven above than the earth beneath, he did not quite expect to ride the whole of the way to England. At Smyrna he took ship, and after some difficulties and dangers, landed at Shoreham, full of joy to behold his four grandchildren, who proved to be five by the time he saw them. The Sussex roads were as bad as need be, and worse than could be anywhere else; but the sturdy oxen set their necks to drag through all things, thick or thin; and the prince stuck fast to his coach, as firmly as the coach stuck fast with him. Having never seen any roads before, he thought them a wonderful institution, and though misled by the light of nature to grumble at some of his worst upsets, a little reflection led him softly back into contentment. A mind "irretrievably analytic"

at once distinguished wisdom's element in the
Sussex reasoners.

" Gin us made thase hyur radds gooder, volk
'ood be radin' down droo 'em avery dai, a'most !
The Lard in heaven never made radds as cud
ever baide the work, if stranngers cud goo along,
wi'out bin vorced to zit down, and mend 'un."

When this was interpreted to his Highness,
he was so struck with its clear sound sense, and
logical sequence, that he fell back, and for the
rest of his journey admired the grandeur of
English character. This sentiment, so deeply
founded, was not likely to be impaired by
further acquaintance with our great nation.
For more than a twelvemonth Prince Agasicles
made his home in England, and many of his
quaint remarks abode on Sussex shepherds'
tongues for generations afterwards, recom-
mended as they were by the vantage of
princely wisdom. For. he picked up quite
enough of the language to say odd things as
a child does, and with a like simplicity. With
this difference, however, that while the great
hits of the little ones, by the proud mother
chronicled, are the lucky outbursts of happy
inexperience, the old man's sage words were
the issue of unhappy experience.

Nevertheless he must have owned a genial nature still at work. For he loved to go down the village lane, when the wind was cold on the highland, and there to wait at a cottage door, till the children came to stare at him. And soon these children had courage to spy that, in spite of his outlandish dress, pockets were about him, and they whispered as much to one another, while their eyes were testing him. At other times when the wind was soft, and shadows of gentle clouds were shed in chase of one another, this great man who had seen the world, and knew all the stars hanging over it—his pleasure was to wander in and out of the ups and downs and nooks of quaintly-plaited hills, and feast his eyes upon their verdure. After that, when the westering light was spreading the upland ridge with gold, and the glades with grey solemnity, this man of declining years was well content to lean on a bank of turf, and watch the quiet ways of sheep. Often thus his mind was carried back to the land of childhood, soothed as in his nurse's arms by nature's peace around him. And if his dreams were interrupted by the crisp fresh sound of browsing, and the ovine tricks as bright as any human exploits, he would turn and do his best to talk with the lonely shepherds.

These, in their simple way, amused him, with their homely saws, and strange content, and independence : and he no less delighted them by unaccustomed modes of speech, and turns of thought beyond their minds, and distant wisdom quite brought home. Thus, and by many other means, this ancient prince, of noble presence, and of flowing snow-white hair, and vesture undisgraced by tailors, left such trace upon these hills, that even his ghost was well believed to know all the sheep-tracks afterwards.

Pleased with England, and with English scenery and customs, as well as charmed with having five quite baby stars to ephemerise, this great astrologer settled to stay in our country as long as possible. He sent his trusty servant, Memel, in a merchant-ship from Shoreham to fetch his implements and papers, precious things of many kinds, and curiosities long in store. Memel brought all these quite safe, except one little thing or two, which he accounted trifles ; but his master was greatly vexed about them.

The prince unpacked his goods most carefully in his own eight-sided room, allowing none but his daughter to help him, and not too sure about trusting her. Then forth he set for a real campaign among the stars of the Southdowns—

and supper-call and breakfast-bell were no more than the bark of a dog to him. And thus he spent his nights, alas! forgetful of the different clime, under the cold stars, when by rights he should have been under the counterpane.

This grew worse and worse, until towards the middle of the month of June, A.D. 1611, his mind was altogether much above the proper temperature. Great things were pending in the heavens, which might be quoted as pious excuse for a little human restlessness. The prince, with his implements always ready, either in his lantern-chamber, or at his favourite spot of the hills, according to the weather, grew more and more impatient daily for the sun to be out of the way, and more and more intolerant every night of any cloudiness. Self-perplexed, downcast, and moody (except when for a few brief hours a brighter canopy changed his gloom into a nervous rapture), he wasted and waned away in body, as his mind grew brighter. After the hurried night, he dragged his faint way home in the morning, and his face of exhausted power struck awe into the household. No one dared to ask him what had happened, or why he looked so; and he like a true philosopher kept all explanations to himself. And then he started anew,

and strode, with his Samian cloak around him,
over the highest, darkest, and most lonesome
hill, out of people's sight.

One place there was which beyond all others
suited his purposes and his mood. A well-
known land-mark now, and the scene of many a
merry picnic, Chanctonbury Ring was then a
lonely spot imbued with terror of a wandering
ghost,—an ancient ghost with a long white
beard, walking even in the afternoon, with its
head bowed down in search of something—a
vain search of centuries.   This long-sought
treasure has now been found ; not by the ghost,
however, but by a lucky stroke of the plough-
share ; and the spectral owner roves no more.
He is supposed, with all the assumption required
to make a certainty, to have been a tenant on
Chancton Manor, under Earl Gurth, the brother
of Harold, and being slain at Hastings, to have
forgotten where his treasure lay.

The Ring, as of old, is a height of vantage
for searching all the country round with a telescope on a breezy day.   It is the salient point and
foreland of a long ridge of naked hills, crowned
with darker eminence by a circle of storm-hud-
dled trees.   But when the astrologer Agasicles
made his principal night haunt here, the Ring

was not overhung with trees, but only outlined by them ; and the rampart of the British camp (if such it were) was more distinct, and uninvaded by planters. So that here was the very place for a quiet sage to make his home, sweeping a long horizon and secure from interruption. To such a citadel of science, guarded by the fame of ghosts, even his daughter Artemise, or his trusty servant Memel, would scarce dare to follow him ; much less any of the peasants, who, from the lowland, seeing a distant light, crossed themselves ; for that fine old custom flourished still among them. Therefore, here his tent was pitched, and here he spent the nights in gazing, and often the days in computation, not for himself, but for his descendants, until his frame began to waste, and his great dark eyes grew pale with it.

CHAPTER VII.

THE LEGEND CONCLUDED.

ARTEMISE, and all around the prince, had been alarmed of late by many little symptoms. He always had been rashly given to take no heed of his food or clothes; but now he went beyond all that, and would have no one take heed for him, or dare to speak of the matter much. Hence, without listening to any nonsense, all the women were sure of one thing—the prince was wearing himself away.

The country people who knew him, and loved him with a little mystery, said it was no wonder that he should worry himself, for being so long away from home, in manners, and in places also. "Sure it must be a trial for him; out all night in the damp and fog; and he no sense of breeches!"

There was much of truth in this, no doubt, as well as much outside it. Yet none of them

could enter into his peculiar state of mind.
So that he often reproached himself for having
been rude, but could not help it. Every one
made allowance for him, as Englishmen do for
a foreigner, as being of a somewhat lower
order, in many ways, in creation. Yet with a
mixture of mind about it, they admired him
more and more.

The largeness of his nature still was very
conspicuous in this,—he never brought his
telescope to bear on his own planet. His
heart was reaching so far forward into future
ages, that he strove to follow downwards nine
or ten entails of stars. To know what was to
become of all that were to be descended from
him ; a highly interesting, but also a deeply
exhausting question. This perpetual effort
told very hard upon his constitution, for nothing
less than fatal worry could have so impaired
his native grace and lofty courtesy.

Yet before his sudden end, a softer and more
genial star was culminant one evening. When
one's time comes to be certain—whether by
earthly senses, or by influence of heaven—of
the buoyant balance turning, and the slender
span outspun, tender thinkings, and kind
wishes, flow to the good side of us. Through

this power, the petty troubles, and the crooked views of life, and the ambition to make others better than we care to be, and every other little turn of wholesome self-deception—these drop off, and leave us sinking into a sense of having lived, and made a humble thing of it.

Whether this be so or not, upon the 18th day of June in the year 1611, Prince Agasicles came home rather hot, and very tired, and fain for a little sleep, if such there were, to wear out weariness. But still he had heavy work left for that night; as a mighty comet had lately appeared, and scared the earth abundantly; yet now he had two or three hours to spare, and they might as well be happy ones. Therefore he sent for his daughter to come, and see to his food and such like, and then to sit with him some few minutes, and to watch the sunset.

Artemise, still young and lovely, knew of course, from Eastern wisdom, that woman's right is to do no wrong. So that she came at once when called, and felt as a mother ought to feel, that she multiplied her obedience vastly, by bringing all her children. Being in a soft state of mind, the old man was glad to see them all, and let them play with him as

freely as childhood's awe of white hair allowed.
Then he laid his hand upon Roger, the heir
of the house, and blessed him on his way to
bed; and after that he had his supper, waited
on by Artemise, who was very grateful for his
kindness to her children. So that she brought
him the right thing, exactly at the right moment, without overcrowding him; and then
she poured him sparkling wine, and comforted
his weary feet, and gave him a delicious pipe
of Persian meconopsis, free from the bane of
opium, yet more dreamy than tobacco. Also
she sprinkled round him delicate attar of the
Vervain (sprightlier and less oppressive than
the scent of roses), until his white beard
ceased to flutter, and the strong lines of his
face relaxed into soft drowsiness.

Observing thence the proper time, when
sweet sleep was encroaching, and haste, and
heat, and sudden temper were as far away as
can be from a man of Eastern blood, Artemise,
his daughter, touched him with the smile which
he used to love, when she was two years old.
and upward; and his thoughts without his
knowledge flew back to her mother.

"Father to me, father dearest," she was
whispering to him, in the native tongue which

charms the old, as having lulled their cradles;
"father to me, tell what trouble has together
fallen on you in this cold and foreign land."

Melody enough was still remaining, in the
most melodious of all mortal languages, for a
child to move a father into softer memories, at
the sound of ancient music thus revived, and
left to dwell.

"Child of my breast," the prince replied, in
the very best modern Hellenic, "a strong desire
to sleep again hath overcome mine intellect."

"Thus is it the more suited, father, for
discourse with such as mine. Let your little
one share the troubles of paternal wisdom."

Suasion more than this was needed, and at
every stage forthcoming, more skilfully than
English words or even looks could render, ere
ever the paternal wisdom might be coaxed to
unfold itself; and even so it was not disposed
to be altogether explicit.

"Ask me no more," he said at last;
"enough that I foresee great troubles overhanging this sad house."

"Oh, father, when, and how, and what?
How shall we get over them, and why should
we encounter them? And will my husband
or my children——"

The prince put up one finger as if to say, "ask one thing at a time," the while he ceased not to revolve many and sad counsels in his venerable head; and in his gaze deep pity mingled with a father's pride and love. Then he spoke three words in a language which she did not comprehend, but retained their sound, and learned before her death that they meant this—"Knowledge of trouble trebles it."

"Now, best-loved father," she exclaimed, perceiving that his face was set to tell her very little, "behold how many helpless ones depend upon my knowledge of the evils I must shield them from. It is—nay, by your eyes—it is the little daughter whom you always cherished with such love and care, who now is the cause of a mind perplexed, as often she has been to you. Father, let not our affairs lay such burden on your mind, but spread them out and lighten it. Often, as our saying hath it, oftentimes the ear of folly is the purse for wisdom's gems."

"I hesitate not, I doubt no longer. I do not divide my mind in twain. The wisdom of them that come after me carries off and transcends mine own, as a mountain doth a half-peck basket. Wherefore, my daughter

Artemise, wife of the noble Englishman with whom she ran away from Caria, and mother of my five grandchildren, she is worthy to know all that I have learned from heaven; ay, and she shall know it all."

"Father to me dearest, yes! Oh, how noble and good of you!"

"She shall know all," continued the prince, with a gaze of ingenuous confidence, and counting on his fingers slowly; "it may be sooner, or it may be later; however, I think one may safely promise a brilliant knowledge of everything in five years after we have completed the second century from this day. But now the great comet is waiting for me. Let me have my boots again. Uncouth, barbarous, frightful things! But in such a country needful."

His daughter obeyed without a word, and hid her disappointment. "It is only to wait till to-morrow," she thought, "and then to fill him a larger pipe, and coax him a little more perhaps, and pour him more wine of Burgundy."

To-morrow never came for him, except in the way the stars come. In the morning he was missed, and sought for, and found dead and cold at the end of his longest telescope.

In Chanctonbury Ring he died, and must have known, for at least a moment, that his death was over him ; for among the stars of his jotting-chart was traced, in trembling charcoal, " Sepeli, ubi cecidi "—" Bury me where I have fallen."

CHAPTER VIII.

ASTROLOGICAL FORECAST.

ALICE LORRAINE, with no small excitement, heard from her father's lips this story of their common ancestor. Part of it was already known to her, through traditions of the country; but this was the first time the whole had been put into a connected narrative. She wondered, also, what her father's reason could be for thus recounting to her this piece of family history, which had never been (as she felt quite sure) confided to her brother Hilary; and, like a young girl, she was saying to herself as he went on—" Shall I ever be fit to compare with that lovely Artemise, my ever-so-long-back grandmother, as the village people call it ? and will that fine old astrologer see that the stars do their duty to us ? and was the great comet that killed him the one that frightens me every night so ? and why did he make such a point of dying without explaining anything?"

However, what she asked her father was a different question from all these.

"Oh, papa, how kind of you to tell me all that story! But what became of Artemise—'Lady Lorraine' I suppose she was?"

"No, my dear; 'Mistress Lorraine,' or 'Madame Lorraine' perhaps they called her. The old earldom had long been lost, and Roger, her son, who fell at Naseby, was the first baronet of our family. But as for Artemise herself—the daughter of the astrologer, and wife of Hilary Lorraine, she died at the birth of her next infant, within a twelvemonth after her father; and then it was known why he had been so reluctant to tell her anything."

"Oh, I am so sorry for her! Then she is that beautiful creature hanging third from the door in the gallery, with ruches beautifully picked out and glossy, and wonderful gold lace on her head, and long hair, and lovely emeralds hanging down as if they were nothing?"

"Yes," said Sir Roland, smiling at his daughter's style of description, "that of course is the lady; and the portrait is clearly a likeness. At one time we thought of naming you after her—"Artemise Lorraine'—for your nurse discovered that you were like her at the mature age of three days."

"Oh, papa, how I wish you had! It would have sounded so much nicer, and so beautifully romantic."

"Just so, my child; and therefore, in these matter-of-fact times, so deliciously absurd. Moreover, I hope that you will not be like her, either in running away from your father, or in any other way—except her kindness and faithfulness."

He was going to say, "in her early death;" but a sudden touch of our natural superstition stopped him.

"Papa, how dare you speak as if any one ever, in all the world, could be fit to compare with you? But now you must tell me one little thing—why have you chosen this very day, which ought to be such a happy one, for telling me so sad a tale, that a little more would have made me cry?"

"The reason, my Lallie, is simple enough. This happens to be the very day when the two hundred years are over; and the astrologer's will, or, whatever the document is, may now be opened."

" His will, papa! Did he leave a will? And none of us ever heard of it!"

" My dear, your acquaintance with his character is, perhaps, not exhaustive. He may have left many wills without wishing to have them published; at any rate, you shall have the chance, before it grows dark, to see what there is."

" Me! or I—whichever is right?—me, or I, to do such a thing! Papa, when I was six years old I could stand on my head; but now I have lost the art, alas!"

" Now, Alice, do try to be sensible, if you ever had such an opening. You know that I do not very often act rashly; but you will make me think I have done so now, unless you behave most steadily."

" Papa, I am steadiness itself; but you must make allowance for a little upset at the marvels heaped upon me."

" My dear child, there are no marvels; or, at any rate, none for you to know. All you have to do is to go, and to fetch a certain document. Whether you know any more about it, is a question for me to consider."

" Oh, papa—to raise me up so, and to cast me down like that! And I was giving you credit for having trusted me so entirely! And very likely you would not even have sent me for this document, if you had your own way about it."

"Alice," Sir Roland answered, smiling at her knowledge of him, "you happen to be particularly right in that conjecture. I should never have thought of sending you to a lonely and forsaken place, if I were allowed to send any one else, or to go myself. And I have not been happy at thinking about it, ever since the morning."

" My father, do you think that I could help rejoicing in such an errand ? It is the very thing to suit me. Where are the keys, papa ? Do be quick."

" I have no intention, my dear child, of hurrying either you or myself. There is plenty of time to think of all things. The sun has not set, and that happens to be one of the little things we have to look to."

"Oh, how very delightful, papa ! That makes it so much more beautiful. And it is the astrologer's room, of course."

" My dear, it strikes me that you look rather pale, in the midst of all your transports. Now, don't go if you are at all afraid."

"Afraid, papa! Now you want to provoke me. You quite forget both my age, it appears, and the family I belong to."

"My pet, you never allow us to be very long forgetful of either of those great facts ; but I trust I have borne them both duly in mind, and I fear that I should even enhance, most needlessly, your self-esteem, if I were to read you the directions which I now am following. For, strangely enough, they do contain predictions as to your character such as we cannot yet perceive (much as we love you) to have come to pass."

"Oh, but who are the 'we,' papa? If everybody knows it—even grandmamma, for instance—what pleasure can I hope to find in ever having been predicted ? "

"You may enjoy that pleasure, Alice, as exclusively as you please. Even your grandmother knows nothing of the matter we have now in hand ; or else—at least I should say perhaps that, if it were otherwise——"

"She would have been down here, of course, papa, and have marched up to the room herself; but, if the whole thing belongs to one's self, nothing can be more delightful than to have been predicted, especially in glowing terms, such as I beg you now, papa, to read in glowing tones to me."

"Alice, I do not like that style of—what shall I call it?—on your part. *Persiflage*, I believe, is the word; and I am glad that there is no English one. It is never graceful in any woman, still less in a young girl like you. Hilary brought it from Oxford first; and perhaps he thought it excellent. Lay it aside now, once and for all. It hopes to seem a clever thing, and it does not even succeed in that."

At these severe words, spoken with a decided attempt at severity, Alice fell back, and could only drop her eyes, and wonder what could have made her father so cross upon his birthday. But, after the smart of the moment, she began to acknowledge to herself that her father was right, and she was wrong. This flippant style was foreign to her, and its charms must be foregone.

"I beg your pardon, father dear," she said, looking softly up at him; "I know that I am not clever, and I never meant to seem so."

"Quite right, Alice; never attempt to do anything impossible." Saying this to her, Sir Roland said to himself that, after all, he should

like to know very much where to find any girl
half so clever as Lallie, or any girl even a
quarter so good, and so loving, and so beautiful.

"The sun is almost gone behind the curve
of the hill, and the scrubby beech, and the nick
cut in the gorsebush. Alice, you know we only
see it for just the Midsummer week like that."

Alice came, with her eyes already quit of
every trace of tears; with vanity and all petty
feelings melting into larger thought. The
beauty of the world would often come around
and overcome her, so that she felt nothing else.

"The sun must always be the same," Sir
Roland said, rather doubtfully, after waiting for
Alice to begin. "No doubt he must always be
the same; but still the great Herschel seems
to think that even the sun is changing. If he
is fed by comets (as our old astronomers used
to say), he ought to be doing very well just
now. Alice, the sun is above ground still,
for people on the hill-top, and there is the
comet already kindling!"

"Of course he is, papa; he never waits for
the sun's convenience. But I must not say
that—I forgot. There would be no English
name for it—would there now, papa?"

"You little tyrant, what troubles I would

inflict upon you if I studied the stars! But I scarcely know the belt of Orion from the Northern Crown. Astronomy does not appear to have taken deep root in our family; but look, there is part of the sun again emerging under Chancton! In five minutes more he will be quite gone; now is the time for me to read these queer directions, which contain so poetical an account of you."

Alice, warned by his former words, and reduced to proper humility, did not speak while her father opened the small strip of parchment, at which she had so long been peeping curiously.

"It is written in Latin," Sir Roland said, "and has been handed from father to son unsealed, and as you see it, from the time of the prince till our time."

"May I see it, papa? What a very clear hand! but you must translate it for me."

"Then here it is:— 'To the father and master of the family of Lorraine, whoever shall be in the year, according to Christian computation, 1811, Agasicles Syennesis, the Carian, bids hail. Do thou, on the 18th day of June, when the sun has well descended, or departed' — *decesserit*, the word is — 'send thy eldest daughter, without any companion, to the astronomer's *cœnaculum*'—why, he never ate supper, the poor old fellow, unless it was the one he died of—'and there let her search in a closet or cupboard'—*in secessu muri*, the words are, as far as I can make out—'and she will find a small document, which to me has been in great price. There will also be something else, to be treated *pro re nata*'—that means according to circumstances—'and according to the orders in the document aforesaid. The virgin will be brave, and beautiful; ready to give herself for the house, and of swiftly-growing prudence. If there be no such virgin then the need for her will not have arisen. It is necessary that no young man should go, and my document must lie hidden for another century. It is not possible that any one of uncertain skill should be certain. But there ought to be a great comet also burning in the sky, of the same complexion as the one that makes my calculations doubtful. Farewell, whosoever thou shalt be, from me descended, and obey me.'"

' "Papa, I declare it quite frightens me. How could he have predicted me, for instance, and this great comet, and even you?"

"Then you think that you answer to your description! My darling, I do believe that you do. But you never shall 'give yourself for the house,' or for fifty thousand houses. Now, will you have anything to do with this strange affair; or will you not? Much rather would I hear you say that you will have nothing to do with it, and that the old man's book may sleep for at least another century."

"Now, papa, you know how much you would be disappointed in me. And do you think that I could have any self-respect remaining? And beside all that, how could I hope to sleep in my bed with all those secrets ever dangling over me?"

"That last is a very important point. With your excitable nature you had better go always through a thing. It was the same with your dear mother. Here are the keys, my daughter. I really feel ashamed to dwell so long on a mere superstition."

CHAPTER IX.

TIIE LEGACY OF THE ASTROLOGER.

THE room known as the Astrologer's (by the maids, less reverently entitled the "star-gazer's closet") was that old eight-sided, or lantern-chamber, which has been mentioned in the short account of the Carian sage and his labours. He had used it alternately with his other quarters in the Chancton Ring; for this had outlook of the rising, as the other had of the setting stars. At the eastern end of the house, it stood away from roofs and chimney-tops, commanding the trending face of hill, and the amplitude of the world below, from north-west round the north and east, to the rising point of Fomahault.

To this room Alice now made her way, as if she had no time to spare. With quick, light steps she passed through the hall, and then the painted library, as it was called from some

old stained glass—and at the further end she
entered a little room with double doors, her
father's favourite musing-place. In the eastern
end of this quiet chamber, and at the eastern
end of all, there was a low and narrow door.
This was seldom locked, because none of the
few who came so far would care to go any
further. For it opened to a small landing-
place, dimly lit, as well as damp, and leading
to a newel staircase, narrow, and made of a
chalky flint, angular and irregular.

Alice stopped to think a little. All things
looked so uninviting that she would rather do
without them. Surely now that the sun had
departed — whether well or otherwise — some
other time would do as nicely for going on
with the business. There was nothing said
of any special hurry, so far as she could
remember; and what could be a more stupid
thing than to try to unlock an ancient door
without any light for the keyhole? She had
a very great mind to go back, and to come
again in the morning.

She turned with a quick turn towards the
light, and the comfort, and the company; then
suddenly she remembered how she had boasted
of her courage; and who would be waiting

to laugh at her, if she came back without her
errand.   Fearing further thought, she ran like
a sunset cloud up the stairway.

Fifty or sixty steps went by her before she
had time to think of them ; a few in the light
of loopholes, but the greater part in governed
gloom, or shadowy mixture flickering.   Then
at the top she stopped to breathe, and recover
her wits, for a moment.   Here a long black
door repelled her—a door whose outside she
knew pretty well, but had no idea of the other
side.   Upon this, she began to think again ;
and her thoughts were almost too much for her.

With a little sigh that would have moved
all imaginable enemies, the swiftly sensitive
girl called up the inborn spirit of her race, and
her own peculiar romance.   These in combi-
nation scarcely could have availed her to turn
the key, unless her father had happened to
think of oiling it with a white pigeon's feather.

When she heard the bolt shoot back, she
made the best of a bad affair.   " In for a
penny, in for a pound ; " "faint heart is fain ; "
" two bites at a cherry ; " and above all, " no-
blesse oblige."   With all these thoughts to
press her forward, in she walked, quite daunt-
lessly.

And lo, there was nothing to frighten her.
Everything looked as old and harmless as the
man who had loved them all ; having made
or befriended them.   His own little lathe, with
its metal bed (cast by himself from a mixture
of his own, defying the rust of centuries),
wanted nothing more than dusting, and some
oil on the bearings.   And the speculum he
had worked so hard at, for a reflecting telescope
—partly his own idea, and partly reflected (as
all ideas are) some years ere the time of
Gregory—the error in its grinding, which had
driven him often to despair, might still. be
traced by an accurate eye through the depth
of two hundred dusty years.   Models, patterns,
moulds, and castings,—many of which would
have shown how slowly our boasted discoveries
have grown,—also favourite tools, and sundry
things past out of their meaning, lay about
among their fellows, doomed alike to do no
work, because the man who had kept them
moving was shorter-lived than they were.

Now young Alice stood among them, in
a reverential way.   They were, of course, no
more than other things laid by to rust, according to man's convenience.   And yet she
could not make up her mind to meddle with

any one of them.   So that she only looked
about, and began to be at home with things.

Her eager mind was always ready to be
crowded with a rash, young interest in all
things.   It was the great fault of her nature
that she never could perceive how very far
all little things should lie beneath her notice.
So that she now had really more than she could
contrive to take in all at once.

But while she, stood in this surprise,
almost forgetting her errand among the mul-
titude of ideas, a cloud above the sunset
happened to be packed with gorgeous light.
Unbosoming itself to the air in the usual
cloudy manner, it managed thereby, to shed
down some bright memories of the departed
one.   And hence there came a lovely gleam of
daylight's afterthought into the north-western
facet of the old eight-sided room.   Alice
crossed this glance of sunset, wondering what
she was to do, until she saw her shadow
wavering into a recess of wall.   There, between the darker windows to the right hand
of the door, a little hover of refraction, striking
upon reflection, because it was fugitive, caught
her eyes.   She saw by means of this a keyhole
in a brightened surface, on a heavy turn of

wall that seemed to have no meaning.   In
right of discovery, up she ran, passed her
fingers over a plate of polished Sussex iron,
and put her key into the hole, of course.

The lock had been properly oiled perhaps,
and put into working order sometimes, even
within the last hundred years.   But still it was
so stiff that Alice had to work the key both
ways, and with both hands, ere it turned.   And
even after the bolt went back, she could not
open the door at once, perhaps because the
jamb was rusty, or the upper hinge had given
forward.   Whatever the hesitation was, the
girl would have no refusal.   She set the key
crosswise in the lock, and drew one corner of
her linen handkerchief through the loop of it,
and then tied a knot, and, with both hands,
pulled.   Inasmuch as her handkerchief was not
made of gauze, or lace, or gossamer, and herself
of no feeble material, the heavy door gave way
at last, and everything lay before her.

"Is that all? oh, is that all?" she cried,
in breathless disappointment, and yet laughing
at herself.   " No jewels, no pearls, no brooches,
or buckles, or even a gold watch!   And the
great Astrologer must have foreseen how sadly,
in this year of our reckoning, I should be

longing for a gold watch! Alas! without it,
what is the use of being 'brave and beautiful'?
Here is nothing more than dust, mouldy old
deeds, and a dirty cushion!"

Alice had a great mind at first to run back
to her father and tell him that, after all, there
was nothing found that would be worth the
carrying. And she even turned, and looked
round the room, to support this strong conclusion. But the weight of ancient wisdom
(pressed on the young imagination by the
stamp of mystery) held her under, and made
her stop from thinking her own thoughts about
it. "He must have known better, of course,
than I do. Only look at his clever tools! I
am sure I could live in this room for a week,
and never be afraid of anything."

But even while she was saying this to
herself, with the mind in command of the
heart, and a fine conscientious courage, there
came to her ears, or seemed to come, a quiet,
low, unaccountable sound. It may have been
nothing, as she tried to think, when first she
began to recover herself; or it may have been
something quite harmless, and most easily
traced to its origin. But whatever it was, in
a moment it managed to quench her desire

to live in that room. With quick hands, now delivered from their usual keen sense of grime, she snatched up whatever she saw in the cupboard, and banged the iron door, and locked it, with a glance of defiant terror over the safer shoulder first, and then over the one that was nearer the noise.

Then she knew she had done her duty very bravely; and that it would be a cruel thing to expect her to stay any longer. And, so to shut out all further views of anything she had no right to see, she slipped back the band of her beautiful hair, and, under that cover, retreated.

CHAPTER X.

A BOY AND A DONKEY.

At this very time there happened to be a boy of no rank, and of unknown order, quietly jogging homeward. He differed but little from other boys; and seemed unworthy of consideration, unless one stopped to consider him. Because he was a boy by no means virtuous, or valiant, neither gifted by nature with any inborn way to be wonderful. Having nothing to help him much, he lived among the things that came around him, to his very utmost; and he never refused a bit to eat, because it might have been a better bit. And now and then, if he got the chance (without any more in the background than a distant view of detection), he had been imagined perhaps to lay hand upon a stray trifle that would lie about, and was due, but not paid, to his merits. Nobody knew where this boy came from, or whether he came at

all indeed, or was only the produce of earth or
sky, at some improper conjuncture.   Nothing
was certain about him ; except that there he
was; and he meant to stay; and people, for
the most part, liked him.   And many women
would have been glad to love him, in a pro-
tective way, but for the fright by all of them
felt, by reason of the magistrates.

These had settled it long ago, at every
kind of session, that this boy (though so comparatively honest) must not be encouraged
much.   He had such a manner of looking
about, after almost anything; and of making
the most of those happy times when luck em-
braces art; above all, he had such exhaustive
knowledge of apple-trees, and potato-buries,
and cows that wanted milking, as well as of
ticklish trout, and occasional little ducks that
had lost their way — that after long-tried
lenience, and allowance for such a neglected
child, justice could no longer take a large and
wholesome view of " Bonny."

Bonny held small heed of justice (even in
the plural number) whenever he could help it.
The nature of his birth and nurture had been
such as to make him take an outside view of
everything.   If people liked him, he liked

them, and would be the last to steal from them ; or at any rate would let them be the last for him to steal from. His inner meaning was so honest, that he almost always waited for some great wrong to be done to him, before he dreamed of making free with almost anybody's ducks.

Widely as he was known, and often glanced at from a wrong point of view, even his lowest detractor could not give his etymology. Many attempted to hold that he might have been called, in some generative outburst, "Bonnie," by a Scotchman of imagination. Others laughed this idea to scorn, and were sure that his right name was "Boney," because of his living in spite of all terror of "Bonyparty." But the true solution probably was (as with all analytic inquiries) the third,—that his right name was "Bony," because his father, though now quite a shadowy being, must have, at some time or other, perhaps, gone about crying, "Rags and Bones, oh!"

These little niceties of origin passed by Bonny as the idle wind. He was proud of his name, and it sounded well ; and wherever he went, the ladies seemed to like him, as an unknown quantity. Also (which mattered far

more to him) the female servants took to him.
And, with many of these, he had such a way,
that it found him in victuals, perhaps twice in
a week.

Nevertheless, he was forced to work as
hard as could be, this summer. The dragging
weight of a hopeless war (as all, except the
stout farmers, now were beginning to consider
it) had been tightening, more and more, the
strain upon the veins of trade, and the burden
of the community.

This good boy lived in the side of a hill,
or of a cliff (as some might call it), white and
beautiful to look at from a proper distance.
Here he had one of those queer old holes,
which puzzle the sagest antiquary, and set him
in fiercest conflict with the even sager geologist.
But in spite of them all, the hole was there;
and in that hole lived Bonny.

Without society, what is life? Our tender-
est and truest affections were not given us for
naught. The grandest of human desires is to
have something or other to wallop; and fate (in
small matters so hard upon Bonny) had known
when to yield, and had granted him this; that is
to say, a donkey.

A donkey of such a clever kind, and so set

up with reasoning powers and a fine heart of
his own, that all his conclusions were almost
right, until they were beaten out of him.   His
name was "Jack," and his nature was of a level
and sturdy order, resenting wrongs, accepting
favours, with all the teeth of gratitude, and
braying (as all clever asses do) at every change
of weather.   His personal appearance also was
noble, striking, and romantic ;   and his face
reminded all beholders of a well-coloured pipe-
bowl upside down.   For all his muzzle and nose ·
were white, as snowy white as if he always
wore a nosebag newly floured from the nearest
windmill.   But just below his eyes, and across
the mace of his jaws, was a ring of brown, and
above that not a speck of white, but deepening
into cloudy blackness throughout all his system.
Then (like the crest of Hector) rose a menacing
frontlet of thick hair, and warlike ears as long as
horns, yet genially revolving ;   and body and
legs, to complete the effect, conceived in the
very best taste to match.

These great virtues of the animal found
their balance in small foibles.   A narrow-minded,
self-seeking vein—a too vindictive memory, an
obstinacy more than asinine, no sense of honour,
and a habit of treating too many questions with

the teeth or heels. These had lowered him
to his present rank; as may be shown hereafter.

To any worked and troubled mind, escaping
into the country, it would have been a treat to
happen (round some corner suddenly, when the
sun throws shadows long) upon Bonny and his
jackass. In the ripe time of the evening, when
the sun is at his kindest, and the earth most
thankful, and the lines of every shadow now are
well accustomed; when the air has summer
hope of never feeling frost again; and every
bush, and tump, and hillock quite knows how to
stand and look; when the creases of yellow
grass, and green grass, by the roadside, leave
themselves for explanation, till the rain shall
settle it; and the thick hedge in the calm air,
cannot rustle, unless it holds a rabbit or a hare
at play,—when all these things, in their quiet
way, guide the shadowy lines of evening, and
the long lanes of farewell, what can soothe the
spirit more than the view of a boy on a
donkey?

Bonny, therefore, was in keeping with the
world around him (as he always contrived to
be) when he came home on Jack, that evening,
from a long day's work at Shoreham. The
lane was at its best almost, with all the wild

flowers that love the chalk, mixed with those that hug the border where the chalk creams into loam. Among them Bonny whistled merrily, as his favourite custom was; to let the Pixies and the Fairies, ere he came under the gloom of the hill, understand that he was coming, and nobody else to frighten them.

Soothed with the beauty of the scene and the majesty of the sunset, Jack drew back his ears and listened drowsily to his master. "Britannia rule the waves" was then the anthem of the nation; and as she seemed to rule nothing else, though fighting very grandly, all patriotic Britons found main comfort in commanding water.

The happiness of this boy and donkey was of that gleeful see-saw chancing, which is the heartiest of all. This has a snugness of its own, which nothing but poverty can afford, and luck rejoice to revel in. As a rich man hugs his shivers, when he has taken a sudden chill, and huddles in over a roaring fire, and boasts that he cannot warm himself, so a poor fellow may cuddle his home, and spread his legs as he pleases, for the sake of its very want of comfort, and the things it makes him think of; all to be hoped for by-and-by. And Bonny was so

destitute, that he had all the world to hope for.
He lived in a hole in the scarp of chalk, at
the foot of the gully of Coombe Lorraine; and
many of his delightful doings might have been
seen from the lofty windows, if any one ever
had thought it worth while to slope a long telescope at him. But nobody cared to look at
Bonny, and scatter his lowly happiness—than
which there is no more fugitive creature, and
none more shy of inspection.

Being of a light and dauntless nature, Bonny
kept whistling and singing his way, over the
grass and through the furze, and in and out the
dappled leafage of the summer evening; while
Jack, with his brightest blinkings, picked the
parts of the track that suited him. The setting
sun was in their eyes, and made them wink
every now and then, and threw the shadow of
long ears, and walking legs, and jogging heads,
here and there and anywhere. Also a very
fine lump of something might in the shadows be
loosely taken to hang across Jack in his latter
parts, coming after Bonny's legs, and choice
things stowed in front of them.

The meaning of this was that they had been
making a very lucky long-shore day, at the
mouth of the river Adur; and on their way

home, had received some pleasing tribute to their many merits in the town of Steyning, and down the road. Jack had no panniers, for his master could not provide such luxuries; but he had what answered as well, or better—a long and trusty meal-sack, strongly stitched at the mouth, and slit for inlet some way down the middle. So that, as it hung well balanced over his sturdy quarters, anything might be popped in quickly; and all the contents must abide together, and churn up into fine tenderness.

As for Bonny himself, the shadows did him strong injustice, such as he was wont to take from all the world, and make light of. The shadows showed him a ragged figure, flapping and flickering here and there, and random in his outlines. But the true glow of the sunset, full upon his face, presented quite another Bonny. No more to be charged as a vagabond than the earth and the sun himself were; but a little boy who loved his home, such as it was, and knew it, and knew little else. Dirty, perhaps, just here and there, after the long dry weather—but if he had been ugly, could he have brought home all that dripping?

To the little fellow himself as yet the question of costume was more important than that of comeliness. And his dress afforded him many sources of pride and self-satisfaction. For his breeches were possessed of inexhaustible vitality, as well as bold and original colour, having been adapted for him by the wife of his great patron, Bottler the pigman, from a pair of Bottler's leggings, made of his own pigskin. The skin had belonged, in the first place, to a very remarkable boar, a thorough Caledonian hog, who escaped from a farm-yard, and lived for months a wild life in St. Leonard's Forest. Here he scared all the neighbourhood, until at last Bottler was invoked to arise like Meleager, and to bring his pig-knife. Bottler met him in single combat, slew him before he had time to grunt, and claiming him as the spoils of war, pickled his hams at his leisure. Then he tanned the hide which was so thick that it never would do for cracklings, and made himself leggings as everlasting as the fame of his exploit.

With these was Bonny now endued over most of his nether moiety. Shoes and stockings he despised, of course, but his little shanks were clean and red, while his shoulders and chest were lost in the splendour of a coachman's crimson waistcoat. At least they were generally so concealed, when he set forth in the

morning, for he picked up plenty of pins, and
showed some genius in arranging them ; but
after a hard day's work, as now, air and light
would always reassert their right of entrance.
Still, there remained enough of the mingled
charm of blush and plush to recall in soft
domestic bosoms bygone scenes, for ever past—
but oh, so sweet among the trays !

To judge him, however, without the fallacy
of romantic tenderness — the breadth of his
mouth, and the turn of his nose, might go a
little way against him. Still, he had such a
manner of showing bright white teeth in a
jocund grin, and of making his frizzly hair stand
up, and his sharp blue eyes express amazement,
at the proper moment ; moreover, his pair of
cheeks was such (after coming off the downs),
and his laugh so dreadfully infectious, and he
had such tales to tell—that several lofty butlers
were persuaded to consider him.

Even the butler of Coombe Lorraine—but
that will come better hereafter. Only as yet
may be fairly said, that Bonny looked up at the
house on the hill with a delicate curiosity ; and
felt that his overtures might have been somewhat ungraceful, or at least ill-timed, when the
new young footman (just taken on) took it

entirely upon himself to kick him all the way
down the hill.   This little discourtesy, doubling
of course Master Bonny's esteem and regard for
the place, at the same time introduced some
constraint into his after intercourse.   For the
moment, indeed, he took no measures to vindi-
cate his honour; although, at a word (as he knew
quite well), Bottler, the pigman, would have
brought up his whip and seen to it.   And even if
any of the maids of the house had been told to
tell Miss Alice about it, Bonny was sure of obtaining justice, and pity, and even half-a-crown.

Quick as he was to forget and forgive the
many things done amiss to him, the boy, when
he came to the mouth of the coombe, looked
pretty sharply about him for traces of that
dreadful fellow, who had proved himself such a
footman.   With Jack to help him, with jaw and
heel, Bonny would not have been so very much
afraid of even him; such a "strong-siding
champion" had the donkey lately shown himself.   Still, on the whole, and after such a long
day's work by sea and shore, the rover was
much relieved to find his little castle unleaguered.

The portal thereof was a yard in height, and
perhaps fifteen inches wide; not all alike, but in
and out, according to the way the things, or the

boy himself, went rubbing it. A holy hermit
once had lived there, if tradition spoke aright.
But if so, he must have been as narrow of body
to get in, as wide of mind to stop there. At
any rate, Bonny was now the hermit, and less of
a saint than a sinner.

The last glance of sunset was being reflected under the eaves of twilight, when these
two came to their home and comfort in the bay
of the quiet land. From the foot of the steep
white cliff, the green sward spread itself with a
gentle slope, and breaks of roughness here and
there, until it met the depth of cornland, where
the feathering bloom appeared—for the summer
was a hot one—reared upon its jointed stalk,
and softened into a silver-grey by the level
touch of evening. The little powdered stars
of wheat-bloom could not now be seen, of
course ; neither the quivering of the awns, nor
that hovering radiance, which in the hot day
moves among them. Still the scent was on
the air, the delicate fragrance of the wheat,
only caught by waiting for it, when the hour
is genial.

Bonny and Jack were not in the humour
now to wait for anything. The scent of the
wheat was nothing to them : but the smell of a

loaf was something. And Jack knew, quite as well as Bonny, that let the time be as hard as it would—and it was a very hard time already, though nothing to what came afterward—nevertheless, there were two white loaves, charmed by their united powers, out of maids who were under notice to quit their situations. Also on their homeward road, they had not failed entirely of a few fine gristly hocks of pork, and the bottom of a skin of lard, and something unknown, but highly interesting, from a place where a pig had been killed that week, much as the time of year was wrong.

"Now, Jack, tend thee'zell," said Bonny, with the air of a full-grown man almost, while he was working his own little shoulders in betwixt the worn hair on the ribs, and the balanced bag overhanging them. Jack knew what he was meant to do; for he brought his white nose cleverly round, just where it was wanted, and pushed it under one end of the bag, and tossed it carefully over his back, so that it slid down beautifully.

When this great bag lay on the ground (or rather, stood up, in a clumsy way, by virtue of what was inside of it), the first thing everybody did was to come, and poke, and sniff at it. And

though the everybody was no more than Bonny
and his donkey, the duty was not badly done,
because they were both so hungry.

When the strings were cut, and the bag in
relief of tension panted, ever so many things
began to ooze, and to ease themselves, out of
it.   First of all two great dollops of oar-weed,
which had excellently performed their task of
keeping everything tight and sweet with the
hungry fragrance of the sea.   Then came a
mixture of almost anything, which a boy of no
daintiness was likely to regard as eatable, or a
child of no science whatever to look upon as a
rarity.   Bonny- was a collector of the grandest
order; the one who collects everything.   Here
was food of the land, and food of the sea, and
food of the tidal river, mingled with food for the
mind of a boy, who had no mind—to his knowledge.   In the humblest way he groped about,
and admired almost everything.

Now he had things. to admire which (in
the heat of the day and the work) had been
caught and stowed away anyhow.   The boy
and the donkey had earned their load with such
true labour that now they could not remember
even half of it.   Jack, by hard collar-work at
the nets; Bonny, by cheering him up the sand,

and tugging himself with his puny shoulders,
and then by dancing, and treading away, and
kicking with naked feet among the wastrel fish,
full of thorns and tails, shed from the vent of
the drag-net by the spent farewell of the shoal-
ing wave.

For, on this very day, there had been the
great Midsummer haul at Shoreham. It was
the old custom of the place ; but even custom
must follow the tides, and the top of the summer
spring-tides (when the fish are always liveliest)
happened, for the year 1811, to come on the
18th day of June. Bonny for weeks had been
looking forward, and now before him lay his
reward !

After many sweet and bitter uses of adver-
sity, this boy, at an early age, had caught the
tail of prudence. It had been to his heart, at
first, a friendly and a native thing, to feast to
the full (when he got the chance) and go empty
away till it came again. But now, being grown
to riper years, and, after much consideration,
declared to be at least twelve years old by the
only pork-butcher in Steyning, Bonny began to
know what was what, and to salt a good deal of
his offal.

For this wise process he now could find a

greater call than usual; because, through the
heat of the day, he had stuck to his first and
firmly-grounded principle—never to refuse refuse. So that many other fine things were
mingled, jumbled, and almost churned, among
the sundry importations of the flowing tide and
net. All of these, now, he well delivered (so
far as sappy limbs could do it) upon a cleanish
piece of ground, well accustomed to such
favours. Then Bonny stood back, with his
hands on his knees, and Jack spread his nose
at some of it.

Loaves of genuine wheaten bread were
getting scarce already. Three or four bad
harvests, following long arrears of discontent,
and hanging on the heavy arm of desperate
taxation, kept the country, and the farmers, and
the people that must be fed, in such a condition
that we (who cannot be now content with anything) deserve no blame when we smack our
lips in our dainty contempt of our grandfathers.

Bonny was always good to Jack, according
to the way they had of looking at one another;
and so, of the choicest spoils, he gave him a
half-peck loaf, of a fibre such as they seldom
softened their teeth with. Jack preferred this
to any clover, even when that luxury could be

won by clever stealing ; and now he trotted away with his loaf to the nearest stump where backing-power against his strong jaws could be got. Here he laid his loaf against the stump, and went a little way back to think about it, and to be sure that every atom was for him. Then, without scruple or time to spare, he tucked up his lips, and began in a hurry to make a bold dash for the heart of it.

" More haste, less speed," is a proverb that seems, at first sight, one of the last that need be impressed upon a donkey. Yet, in the present instance, Jack should have spared himself time to study it ; for in less than a moment he ran up to Bonny, with his wide mouth at its widest, snorting with pain, and much yearning to bellow, but by the position disabled. There was something stuck fast in the roof of his mouth, in a groove of the veiny black arches ; and work as he might with his wounded tongue, he was only driving it further in. His great black eyes, as he gasped with fright, and the piteous whine of his quivering nose, and his way altogether so scared poor Bonny, that the chances were he would run away. And so, no doubt, he must have done (being but a little boy as yet), if it had not chanced that a flash

of something caught his quick eye suddenly,
something richly shining in the cavern of the
donkey's mouth.

This was enough, of course, for Bonny.
His instinct of scratching, and digging, and
hiding was up and at work in a moment. He
thrust his brown hand between Jack's great
jaws, and drew it back quickly enough to escape
the snap of their glad reunion. And in his
hand was something which he had drawn from
the bag of the net that day, but scarcely stopped
to look at twice, in the huddle of weeds and the
sweeping. It had lain among many fine gifts
of the sea—skates, and dog-fish, sea-devils,
sting-rays, thornbacks, inky cuttles, and scol-
lops, cockles, whelks, green crabs, jelly-fish, and
everything else that makes fishermen swear,
and then grin, and then spit on their palms
again. Among these in Bonny's bag had lain
manifold boons of the life-giving earth, extracted
from her motherly feeling by one or two good
butchers.

Bonny made no bones of this. Fish, flesh,
fowl, or stale red-herring—he welcomed all
the works of charity with a charitable nose,
and fingers not of the nicest. So that his
judgment could scarcely have been "prejudi-

cially affected by any preconceived opinion "—— as our purest writers love to say—when he dropped this thing, and smelled his thumb, and cried, " Lord, how it makes my hands itch ! "

After such a strong expression, what can we have to say to him? It is the privilege of our period to put under our feet whatever we would rather not face out. At the same time, to pretend to love it, and lift it by education. Nevertheless, one may try to doubt whether poor Bonny's grandchildren (if he ever presumed to have any) thrive on the lesson, as well as he did on the loaf, of charity.

CHAPTER XI.

CHAMBER PRACTICE.

THERE used to be a row of buildings, well within the sacred precincts of the Inner Temple, but still preserving a fair look-out on the wharves, and the tidal gut at their back, till the whole view was swallowed by gas-works. Here for long ages law had flourished on the excrete things of outlawry, fed by the reek of Whitefriars, as a good nettle enjoys the mixen.

Already, however, some sweeping changes had much improved this neighbourhood; and the low attorneys who throve on crime, and of whom we get unpleasant glimpses through our classic novelists, had been succeeded by men of repute, and learning, and large practice. And among all these there was not one more widely known and respected than Glanvil Malahide, K.C.; an eminent equity-barrister, who now declined to don the wig in any ordinary cause.

He had been obliged, of course, to fight, like the rest of mankind, for celebrity; but as soon as this was well assured, he quitted the noisier sides of it. But his love of the subtleties of the law (spun into fairer and frailer gossamer by the soft spider of equity), as well as the power of habit, kept him to his old profession; so that he took to chamber practice, and had more than he could manage.

Sir Roland Lorraine had known this gentleman by repute at Oxford, when Glanvil Malahide was young, and believed to be one of the best scholars there; in the days when scholarship often ripened (as it seldom does now) to learning. For the scholarship now must be kept quite young, for the smaller needs of tuition.

Hence it came to pass that as soon as Hilary Lorraine was quite acquit of Oxford leadingstrings, and had scrambled into some degree, his father, who especially wished (for some reasons of his own) to keep the boy out of the army, entered him gladly among the pupils of Mr. Glanvil Malahide. Not that Hilary was expected ever to wear the horse-hair much (unless an insane desire to do so should find its way into his open soul), but that the excellent goodness of law might drop, like the gentle dew from heaven, and grow him into a Justice of the Peace.

Hilary looked upon this matter, as he did on too many others, with a sweet indifference. If he could only have had his own way, he would have been a soldier long ago ; for that was the time when all the spirit of Britain was roused up to arms. But this young fellow's great fault was, to be compact of so many elements that nothing was settled amongst them. He had "great gifts," as Mr. Malahide said—"extraordinary talents," we say now—but nobody knew (least of all their owner) how to work them properly. This is one of the most unlucky compositions of the human mind—to be applicable to everything, but applied to nothing. If Hilary had lain under pressure, and been squeezed into one direction, he must have become a man of mark.

This his father could not see. As a general rule a father fails to know what his son is fit for ; and after disappointment, fancies (for a little time at least) himself a fool to have taken the boy to be all that the mother said of him. Nevertheless, the poor mother knows how right she was, and the world how wrong.

But Hilary Lorraine, from childhood, had
no mother to help him. What he had to help
him was good birth, good looks, good abilities,
a very sweet temper, and a kind and truly
genial nature. Also a strongish will of his
own (whenever his heart was moving), yet
ashamed to stand forth boldly in the lesser
matters. And here was his fatal error; that
he looked upon almost everything as one of the
lesser matters. He had, of course, a host of
friends, from the freedom of his manner; and
sometimes he would do such things that the
best, or even the worst of them, could no longer
walk with him. Things not vicious, but a great
deal too far gone in the opposite way—such as
the snatching up of a truly naked child and
caressing it, or any other shameful act, in the
face of the noblest Christendom. These things
he would do, and worse; such as no toady with
self-respect could smile at in broad daylight,
and such as often exposed the lad to laughter·
in good society. One of his best friends used
to say that Hilary wanted a vice or two to
make his virtues balance. This may have
been so; but none the less, he had his share
of failings.

For a sample of these last, he had taken

up and made much of one of his fellow-pupils
in these well-connected chambers. This was
one Gregory Lovejoy, a youth entirely out of
his element among fashionable sparks. Steadfast ambition of a conceptive mother sent him,
against his stars, to London; and here he became the whetstone for those brilliant blades,
his fellow-pupils; because he had been at no
university, nor even so much as a public school,
and had no introduction to anybody who had
never heard of him.

Now the more the rest disdained this fellow,
the more Lorraine regarded him; feeling, with
a sense too delicate to arise from any thought,
that shame was done to good birth by being even
conscious of it, except upon great occasions.
And so, without giving much offence, or pretending to be a champion, Hilary used to shield
young Lovejoy from the blunt shafts of small
humour continually levelled at him.

Mr. Malahide's set of chambers was perhaps
the best to be found in Equity Walk, Inner
Temple. His pupils—ten in number always,
because he would accept no more, and his high
repute insured no less—these worthy youths
had the longest room, facing with three whitey-
brown windows into " Numa Square." Hence

the view, contemning all "utilitarian edifices,"
freely ranged, across the garden's classic walks
of asphodel, to the broad Lethean river on
whose wharves we are such weeds.   For
" Paper Buildings," named from some swift
sequence of suggestion, reared no lofty height
as yet to mar the sedentary view.

All who have the local key will enter into
the scene at once ; so far, at least, as necessary
change has failed to operate.   But Mr. Malahide's pupils scarcely ever looked out of the
windows.   None, however, should rashly blame
them for apathy as to the prospect.   They
seldom looked out of the windows, because they
were very seldom inside them.

In the first place, their attendance there was
voluntary and precarious.   They paid their
money, and they took their choice whether they
ever did anything more.   Each of them paid—
or his father for him—a fee of a hundred
guineas to have the " run of the chambers," and
most of them carried out their purpose by a
runaway from them.   The less they came, the
less trouble they caused to Mr. Glanvil Malahide ; who always gave them that much to
know, when they paid their fee of entrance.
" If you mean to be a lawyer," he said, " I will

do my best to make you one. If you only come for the name of it, I shall say but little more to you." This, of course, was fair enough, and the utmost that could be expected of him: for most of his pupils were young men of birth, or good position in the English counties, to whom in their future condition of life a little smattering of law, or the credit of owning such smattering, would be worth a few hundred guineas. Common Law, of course, was far more likely to avail them, in their rubs of the world, than equity; but of that fine drug they had generally taken their dose in Pleaders' Chambers, and were come to wash the taste away in the purer shallows of equity.

Hilary, therefore, might be considered, and certainly did consider himself, a remarkably attentive pupil, for he generally was to be found in chambers four or even five days of the week, coming in time to read all the news, before the five o'clock dinner in Hall. Whereas the Honourable Robert Gumption, and Sir Francis Kickabout, two of his fellow-pupils, had only been seen in chambers once since they paid their respective fees; and the reason of their attendance then was that they found the towels too dirty to use at the billiard-rooms in Fleet

Street. The clerks used to say among themselves, that "these young fellows must be dreadful fools to pay one hundred guineas, because any swell with the proper cheek might easy enough have the go of the chambers, and nobody none the wiser; for they wouldn't know him, nor the other young gents, and least of all old "horsewig."

However, there chanced to be two or three men who made something more than a very expensive lounge of these eminent chambers. Of these worthy fellows, Rice Cockles was one (who had been senior wrangler two years before, and from that time knew not one good night's rest, till the Woolsack broke his fall into his grave), and another was Gregory Lovejoy. Cockles was thoroughly conscious—as behoves a senior wrangler—of possessing great abilities; and Lovejoy knew, on his own behalf, that his mother at least was as sure as could be of all the wonders he must do.

Hilary could not bear Rice Cockles, who was of a dry sarcastic vein; but he liked young Lovejoy more and more, the more he had to defend him. Youths who have not had the fortune to be at a public school or a college seldom know how to hold their tongues, until

the world has silenced them. Gregory, therefore, thought no harm to boast opportunely one
fine May morning (when some one had seen a
tree blossoming somewhere) of the beauty of his
father's cherry-trees. How noble and grand
they must be just now, one sheet of white, white,
white, he said, as big as the Inner and the
Middle Temple and Lincoln's Inn, all put
together! And then how the bees were among
them buzzing, knowing which sorts first to milk;
and the tortoise-shell butterflies quite sure to be
out, for the first of their summering. But in the
moonlight, best of all, when the moon was three
days short of full, then was the time an unhappy
Londoner must be amazed with happiness.
Then to walk among them was like walking in
a fairy-land, or being lost in a sky of snow,
before a flake begins to fall. A delicate soft
world of white, an in-and-out of fancy lace, a
feeling of some white witchery, and almost a
fright that little white blossoms have such
power over one.

"Where may one find this grand paradise?"
asked Rice Cockles, as if he could scarcely
refrain his feet from the road to it.

"Five miles the other side of Sevenoaks,"
Gregory answered, boldly.

"I know the country. Does your father grow cherries for Covent Garden market?"

"Of course he does. Didn't you know that?" Thenceforth in chambers Lovejoy was always known as "Cherry Lovejoy." And he proudly answered to that name.

It was now the end of June, and the cherries must be getting ripe. The day had been very hot and sultry, and Hilary came into chambers later than his usual time, but fresh as a lark, as he always was. Even Mr. Malahide had felt · the weight of the weather, and of his own threescore years and five, and in his own room was dozing. The three clerks, in their little den, were fit for next to nothing, except to lie far away in some meadow, with sleepy beer, under alder-trees. Even Rice Cockles had struck work with one of those hopeless headaches which are bred by hot weather from satire, a thing that turns sour above freezing-point; and no one was dwelling in the long hot room save the peaceful and steady Gregory.

Even he, with his resolute will to fulfil his mother's prophecies, could scarcely keep his mind from flagging, or his mouth from yawning, as he went through some most elaborate answer to a grand petition in equity—the iniquity being, to a common mind, that the question could have arisen. But Mr. Malahide, of course, regarded things professionally.

"Lovejoy, thy name is 'Love misery,'" cried young Lorraine, who never called his fellow-pupil "Cherry," though perfectly welcome to do so. "I passed an optician's shop just now, and the thermometer stands at 96°. That quill must have come from an ostrich to be able to move in such weather. Even the Counsellor yields to the elements. Hark how he winds his sultry horn! Is it not a great and true writer who says, 'I tell thee that the quills of the law are the deadliest shafts of the Evil One'? Come, therefore, and try a darting match."

Gregory felt no inclination for so hot a pastime; he had formed, however, a habit of yielding to the impulsive and popular Hilary; which led him into a few small scrapes, and one or two that were not small. Lorraine's unusual brightness of nature, and personal beauty, and gentle bearing, as well as an inborn readiness to be pleased with everybody, insured him a good liking with almost all kinds of people. How then could young Lovejoy, of a fine but

unshapen character, and never introduced to
the very skirts of good society, help looking up
to his champion Hilary as a charming deity?
Therefore he made way at once for Hilary's
sudden freak for darts. The whole world
being at war just then (as happens upon the
average in every generation), Cherry Lovejoy
slung his target, a legal almanac for the year.
Then he took four long quills, and pared them
of their plumes, and split the shafts, and fitted
each with four paper wings, cut and balanced
cleverly. His aptness in the business showed
that this was not his first attempt; and it was
a hard and cruel thing that he should now have
to prepare them. But the clerks had a regular
trick of stealing the "young pups'" darts from
their unlocked drawers, partly for practice
among themselves, but mainly to please their
families.

"Capital! Beautifully done!" cried Hilary,
as full of life as if the only warmth of the
neighbourhood were inside him. "We never
turned out such a good lot before; I could
never do that like you. But now for the tips,
my dear fellow!"

"Any fool can do what I have done. But
no one can cut the tip at all, to stick in the

target, and not bounce back; only you, Mr. Lorraine."

"Mister Lorraine! now, Gregory Lovejoy, I thought we liked one another well enough to have dropped that long ago. If you will only vouchsafe to notice, you shall see how I cut the tip, so that the well-sped javelin pierces even a cover of calf-skin." It was done in a moment, by some quick art, inherited, perhaps, from Prince Agasicles; and then they took their stations.

From the further end of the room they cast (for thirty feet and more perhaps) over two great tables scarred by keen generations of lawyers. Hilary threw the stronger shaft, but Gregory took more careful aim; so that in spite of the stifling heat, the contest grew exciting.

"Blest if they young donkeys knows hot from cold!" said the senior clerk, disturbed in his little room by the prodding and walking, and the lively voices.

"Sooner them, than you nor me!" the second clerk muttered sleepily. When the most un-grammatical English is wanted, a copying clerk is the man to supply it.

In spite of unkindly criticism, the brisk

acontic strife went on. And every hit was
chronicled on a long sheet of draft paper.

"Sixteen to you, eighteen to me!" cried
Gregory, poising his long shadowed spear,
while his coat and waistcoat lay in the folds of
a suit that could never terminate, and his square
Kentish face was even redder than a ripe May-
Duke. At that moment the door was opened,
and in came Mr. Malahide.

"Just so!" he said, in his quiet way; "I
now understand the origin of a noise which has
often puzzled me. Lorraine, what a baby you
must be!"

"Can a baby do that?" said Hilary, as he
stepped into poor Gregory's place, and sped his
dart into the Chancellor's eye, the bull's-eye of
their target.

"That was well done," Mr. Malahide
answered; "perhaps it is the only good shot
you will ever make in your profession."

"I hope not, sir. Under your careful tuition
I am laying the foundations of a mighty host of
learning."

At this the lawyer was truly pleased. He
really did believe that he took some trouble
with his pupils; and his very kind heart was
always gratified by their praises. And he

showed his pleasure in his usual way by harping
on verbal niceties.

" Foundations of a host, Lorraine! Foundations of a pile, you mean; and as yet, *lusisti
pilis.* But you may be a credit to me yet.
Allowance must be made for this great heat.
I will talk to you to-morrow."

With these few words, and a pleasant smile,
the eminent lawyer withdrew to his den, feign-
ing to have caught no glimpse of the deeply-
blushing Lovejoy. For he knew quite well
that Gregory could not afford to play with his
schooling; and so (like a proper gentleman) he
fell upon the one who could. Hilary saw his
motive, and with his usual speed admired him.

"What a fine fellow he is!" he said, as if in
pure self-commune; "from the time he becomes
Lord Chancellor, I will dart at no legal almanac.
But the present fellow—however, the weather
is too hot to talk of him. Lovejoy, wilt thou
come with me? I must break out into the
country."

"What!" cried Gregory, drawing up at the
magic word from his stool of repentance, and
the desk of his diminished head. "What was
that you said, Lorraine?"

"Fair indeed is the thing thou hast said,

and fair is the way thou saidst it.   Tush ! shall
I never get wholly out of my ignorant knowledge of Greek plays ?   Of languages that be,
or have been, only two words survive this
weather, in the streets of London town; one is
'rus,' and the other 'country.'"

"'It is a sweet and decorous thing to die
on behalf of the country.'   That line I remember well; you must have seen it somewhere ?"

"It is one of my earliest memories, and not
a purely happy one.   But that is 'patria,' not
'rus.'   'Patria' is the fatherland; 'rus' is a
fellow's mother.   None can understand this
parable till they have lived in London."

"Lorraine," said Gregory, coming up shyly,
yet with his brown eyes sparkling, and a steadfast mouth to declare himself, "you are very
much above me, of course, I know."

"I am uncommonly proud to hear it," Hilary
answered, with his most sweet smile, "because
I must be a much finer fellow than I ever could
have dreamed of being."

"Now, you know well enough what I mean.
I mean, in position of life, and all that, and birth,
and society—and so on."

"To be sure," said Hilary gravely, making

a trumpet of blotting paper; "any other advantage, Gregory?"

"Fifty, if I could stop to tell them. But I see that you mean to argue it. Now, argument is a thing that always——"

"Now, Gregory, just acknowledge me your superior in argument, and I will confess myself your superior in every one of those other things."

"Well, you know, Lorraine, I could scarcely do that. Because it was only the very last time——"

"Exactly," said Hilary; "so it was—the very last time, you left me no more than a shadow caught in a cleft stick. Therefore, friend Gregory, say your say, without any traps for the sole of my foot."

"Well, what I was thinking was no more than this—if you would take it into consideration now—considering what the weather is, and all the great people gone out of London, and the streets like fire almost, and the lawyers frightened by the comet, quite as if, as if, almost——"

"As if it were the devil come for them."

"Exactly so. Bellows' clerk told me, after he saw the comet, that he could prove he had

never been articled. And when you come to
consider also that there will be a row to-morrow
morning—not much, of course, but still a thing
to be avoided till the weather cools—I thought;
at least, I began to think——"

"My dear fellow, what? Anxiety in this
dreadful weather is fever."

"Nothing, nothing at all, Lorraine. But
you are the sweetest-tempered fellow I ever
came across; and so I thought that you would
not mind—at least, not so very much, perhaps——"

"My sweet temper is worn out. I have no
mind to mind anything, Gregory; come and
dine with me."

"That is how you stop me always, Lorraine;
I cannot be for ever coming, and come, to dine
with you. I always like it; but you know——"

"To be sure, I know that I like it too. It
is high time to see about it. Who could dine
in Hall to-day, and drink his bottle of red-hot
port?"

"I could, and so could a hundred others.
And I mean to do it, unless——"

"Unless what? Mysterious Gregory, by
your face I know that you have some very fine
thing to propose. Have you the heart to

keep me suspended, as well as uncommonly
hungry?"

"It is nothing to make a fuss about. Lorraine, you want to get out of town, for a little
wholesome air. I want to do the same; and
something came into my head quite casually."

"Such things have an inspiration. Out
with it at last, fair Gregory."

"Well, then, if you must have it, how I
should like for you to come with me to have a
little turn among my father's cherry-trees!"

"What a noble thought!" said Hilary; "a
poetic imagination only could have hit on such
a thought. The thermometer at 96°—and the
cherries—can they be sour now?"

"Such a thing is quite impossible," Gregory
answered gravely; "in a very cold, wet summer
they are sometimes a little middling. But in
such a splendid year as this, there can be no
two opinions. Would you like to see them?"

"Now, Lovejoy, I can put up with much;
but not with maddening questions."

"You mean, I suppose, that you could enjoy
half-a-dozen cool red cherries, if you had the
chance to pick them in among the long green
leaves?"

"Half-a-dozen! Half-a-peck; and half-a-bushel afterwards. Where have I put my hat? I am off, if it costs my surviving sixpence."

"Lorraine, all the coaches are gone for the day. But you are always in such a hurry. You ought to think a little, perhaps, before you make up your mind to come. Remember that my father's house is a good house, and as comfortable as any you could wish to see; still it may be different from what you are accustomed to."

"Such things are not worth thinking about. Custom, and all that, are quite below contempt; and we are beginning to treat it so. The greatest mistake of our lives is custom; and the greatest delight is to kick it away. Will your father be glad to see me?"

"He has heard me talk of you, many a time; and he would have been glad to come to London (though he hates it so abominably), to see you and to ask you down, if he thought that you would require it. It is a very old-fashioned place; you must please to bear that in mind. Also, my father, and my mother, and all of us, are old-fashioned people, living in a quiet way. You would carry on more in an hour, than we do in a twelvemonth. We like to go all over things, ever so many times, perhaps (like pushing

rings up and down a stick), before we begin to
settle them. But when we have settled them,
we never start again ; as you seem to do."

"Now, Gregory, Gregory, this is bad.
When did you know me to start again?
Ready I am to start this once, and to dwell
in the orchards for ever."

In a few words more, these two young fellows agreed to take their luck of it. There was
nothing in chambers for Lovejoy to lose, by
going away for a day or two ; and Hilary long
had felt uneasy at leaving a holiday overdue.
Therefore they made their minds up promptly
for an early start next morning, ere the drowsy
town should begin to kick up its chimney-pots,
like a sluggard's toes.

"Gregory," said Lorraine, at last, "your
mind is a garden of genius. We two will sit·
upon bushel-baskets, and watch the sun rise out
of sacks. Before he sets, we will challenge him
to face our early waggon. Covent Garden is
our trysting spot, and the hour 4 a.m. Oh, day
to be marked with white chalk for ever !"

"I am sure I can't tell how that may be,"
answered the less fervent Gregory. "There is
no chalk in our grounds at all; and I never saw
black chalk anywhere. But can I trust you to

be there ? If you don't come, I shall not go without you; and the whole affair must be put off."

"No fear, Gregory; no fear of me. The lark shall still be on her nest;—but wait, my friend, I will tell the Counsellor, lest I seem to dread his face."

Lovejoy saw that this was the bounden duty of a gentleman, inasmuch as the learned lawyer had promised his young friend a little remonstrance upon the following morning. The chances were that he would forget it; and this, of course, enhanced the duty of making him remember it. Therefore Hilary gave three taps on the worm-eaten door of his good tutor, according to the scale of precedence. This rule was—inferior clerk, one tap; head-clerk, two taps; pupil (being no clerk at all, and paying, not drawing, salary), as many taps as he might think proper, in a reasonable way.

Hilary, of course, began, as he always managed to begin, with almost everybody.

"I am sorry to disturb you, sir; and I have nothing particular to say."

"In that case, why did you come, Lorraine ? It is your usual state of mind."

"Well, sir," said Hilary, laughing at the

terse mood of the master, "I thought you had something to say to me—a very unusual state of mind," he was going to say, "on your part;" but stopped, with a well-bred youth's perception of the unbecoming.

"Yes, I have something to say to you. I remember it now, quite clearly. You were playing some childish game with Lovejoy, in the pupil's room. Now, this is all well enough for you; who are fit for nothing else, perhaps. Your father expects no work from you; and if he did, he would never get it. You may do very well, in your careless way, being born to the gift of indifference. But those who can and must work hard—is it honest of you to entice them? You think that I speak severely. Perhaps I do, because I feel that I am speaking to a gentleman."

"It is uncommonly hard," said Hilary, with his bright blue eyes half conscious of a shameful spring of moisture, "that a fellow always gets it worse for trying to be a gentleman."

"You have touched a great truth," Mr. Malahide answered, labouring heavily not to smile; "but so it always must be. My boy, I am sorry to vex you; but to be vexed is better than to grieve. You like young Lovejoy—don't make him idle."

"Sir, I will dart at him henceforth, whenever I see him lazy; instead of the late Lord Chancellor, now sitting upon asphodel."

"Lorraine," the great lawyer suddenly asked, in a flush of unusual interest, "you have been at Oxford quite recently. They do all sorts of things there now. Have they settled what asphodel is?"

"No, sir, I fear that they never will. There are several other moot questions still. But with your kind leave, I mean to try to settle that point to-morrow."

CHAPTER XII.

MARTIN LOVEJOY, Gregory's father, owned and
worked a pleasant farm in that part of Kent
which the natives love to call the "Garden of
Eden." In the valley of the upper Medway,
a few miles above Maidstone, pretty hamlets
follow the soft winding of the river. Here an
ancient race of settlers, quiet and intelligent,
chose their home, and chose it well, and love it
as dearly as ever.

To argue with such people is to fall below
their mercy. They stand at their cottage-doors,
serenely as thirty generations of them have stood.
A riotous storm or two may have swept them;
but it never lasted long. The bowers of hop
and of honeysuckle, trimmed alleys, and rambling roses, the flowering trees by the side of
the road, and the truest of true green meadows,
the wealth of deep orchards retiring away—as

all wealth does—to enjoy itself; and where
the land condescends to wheat, the vast gratitude of the wheat-crop,—nobody wonders, after
a while, that these men know their value.

The early sun was up and slurring light
upon London housetops, as a task of duty only,
having lost all interest in a thing even he can
make no hand of. But the brisk air of the
morning, after such a night of sweltering, and
of strong smells under slates, rode in the perpetual balance of the clime, and spread itself.
Fresh, cool draughts of new-born day, as vague
as the smile of an infant, roved about; yet were
to be caught according to the dew-lines. And
of these the best and truest followed into
Covent Garden, under the force of attraction
towards the green stuff they had dwelt among.

Here was a wondrous reek of men before
the night had spent itself. Such a Babel,
of a market-morning in the "berry-season," as
makes one long to understand the mother-
tongue of nobody. Many things are nice and
handsome; fruit and flowers are fair and fresh;
life is as swift as life can be; and the pulse of
price throbs everywhere. Yet, upon the whole,
it is wiser not to say much more of it.

Martin Lovejoy scarcely ever ventured into

this stormy world.   In summer and autumn he
was obliged to send some of his fruit to London;
but he always sent it under the care of a trusty
old retainer, Master John Shorne, whose crusty
temper and crisp wit were a puzzle to the
Cockney costermonger.   Throughout the market, this man was known familiarly as "Kentish
Crust," and the name helped him well in his
business.

Now, in the summer morning early, Hilary
Lorraine, with his most sprightly walk and
manner, sought his way through the crowded
alleys and the swarms of those that buy and
sell.   Even the roughest of rough customers
(when both demand and supply are rough),
though they would not yield him way, at any
rate did not shove him by.   "A swell, to buy
fruit for his sweetheart," was their conclusion in
half a glance at him.   "Here, sir, here you are!
berries for nothing, and cherries we pays you
for eating of them!".

With the help of these generous fellows,
Hilary found his way to John Shorne and the
waggon.   The horses, in unbuckled ease, were
munching their well-earned corn close by; for
at that time Covent Garden was not squeezed
and driven as now it is.   The tail-board of the

waggon was now hanging upon its hinges, and
" Kentish Crust," on his springy rostrum, dealt
with the fag-end of his goods. The market, in
those days, was not flooded with poor foreign
produce, fair to the eye, but a fraud on the belly,
and full of most dangerous colic. Englishmen,
at that time, did not spend their keenest wits
upon the newest and speediest measures for
robbing their brother Englishmen ; and a native
would really buy from his neighbour as gladly
as from his born enemy.

Master John Shorne had a canvas bag on
the right side of his breeches, hanging outside,
full in sight, defying every cut-purse. · That age
was comparatively honest ; nevertheless, John
kept a club, cut in Mereworth wood, quite
handy. And, at every sale he made, he rang
his coin of the realm in his bag, as if he were ·
calling bees all round the waggon. This generally led to another sale. For money has a
richly irresistible joy in jingling.

Hilary was delighted to watch these things,
so entirely new to him. He had that fatal gift
of sliding into other people's minds, and
wondering what to do there. Not as a great
poet has it (still reserving his own strength, and
playing on the smaller nature kindly as he loves

it), but simply as a child rejoices to play with other children. So that he entered eagerly into the sudden changes of John's temper, according to the tone, the bidding, and, most of all, the importance of the customers that came to him. By this time the cherries were all sold out, having left no trace except some red splashes, where an over-ripe sieve had been bleeding. But the Kentish man still had some bushels of peas, and new potatoes, and bunches of cole-worts, and early carrots, besides five or six dozens of creamy cauliflowers, and several scores of fine-hearted lettuce. Therefore he was dancing with great excitement up and down his van, for he could not bear to go home un-cleared; and some of his shrewder customers saw that by waiting a little longer they would be likely to get things at half-price. Of course, he was fully alive to this, and had done his best to hide surplus stock, by means of sacks, and mats, and empty bushels piled upon full ones.

"Crusty, thou must come down, old fellow," cried a one-eyed costermonger, winking first at John, and then through the rails, and even at the springs of the van; "half the load will go back to Kent, or else to the cowkeeper, if so be you holds on so almighty dear."

"Ha, then, Joe, are you waiting for that? Go to the cow-yard and take your turn. They always feeds the one-eyed first. Gentlemen, now—while there's anything left! We've kept all the very best back to the last, 'cos they chanced to be packed by an Irishman. 'First goes in, must first come out.' Paddy, are you there to stick to it?"

"Be jabers, and how could I slip out, when the hape of you was atop of me? And right I was, be the holy poker; there it all is the very first in the bottom of the vhan!"

"Now, are you nearly ready, John!" asked Gregory, suddenly appearing through the laughter of the crowd; "here is the gentleman going with us, and I can't have him kept waiting."

"Come up, Master Greg, and help sell out, if you know the time better than I do." John Shorne was vexed, or he would not so have spoken to his master's son.

To his great surprise, with a bound up came not Gregory Lovejoy, who was always a little bit shy of the marketing, but Hilary Lorraine, declared by dress and manner (clearly marked, as now they never can be) of an order wholly different from the people round him.

"Let me help you, sir," he said; "I have long been looking on; I am sure that I understand it."

"Forty years have I been at 'un, and I scarcely knows 'un now. They takes a deal of mannerin', sir, and the prices will go in and out."

"No doubt; and yet for the sport of it, let me help you, Master Shorne. I will not sell a leaf below the price you whisper to me."

In such height of life and hurry, half a minute is enough to fetch a great crowd anywhere. It was round the market in ten seconds that a grand lord was going to sell out of Grower Lovejoy's waggon. For a great wager, of course it must be; and all who could rush, rushed to see. Hilary let them get ready, and waited till he saw that their money was burning. Meanwhile Crusty John was grinning one of his most experienced grins.

"Don't let him; oh, don't let him," Gregory shouted to the salesman, as Hilary came to the rostrum with a bunch of carrots in one hand and a cauliflower in the other—"What would his friends say if they heard it?"

"Nay, I'll not let 'un," John Shorne answered, mischievously taking the verb in its (now) pro-

vincial sense ; " why should I let 'un ?   It can't
hurt he, and it may do good to we."

In less than ten minutes the van was cleared,
and at such prices as Grower Lovejoy's goods
had not fetched all through the summer.   Such
competition arose for the honour of purchasing
from a " nobleman," and so enchanted were the
dealers' ladies, many of whom came thronging
round, with Hilary's bright complexion, gay
address, and complaisancy.

" Well done, my lord ! well done indeed ! "
Crusty John, to keep up the fiction, shouted
when he had pouched the money—" Gentlemen
and ladies, my lord will sell again next week ;
he has a heavy bet about it with the Prince
Reg——tush, what a fool I am ! they will send
me to prison if I tell ! "

As a general rule, the more suspicious
people are in some ways, the more credulous
are they in all the rest.   Kentish Crust was
aware of this, and expected and found for the
next two months extraordinary inquiry for his
goods.

" Friend Gregory, wherefore art thou glum ? "
said Hilary to young Lovejoy, while the horses
with their bunched-up tails were being buckled
to again.   Lorraine was radiant with joy, both

at his recent triumph in a matter quite unknown
to him, and even more because of many little
pictures spread before him by his brisk imagination far away from London.   Every stamp of
a horse's hoof was as good as a beat of the
heart to him.

"Lorraine," the sensible Gregory answered,
after some hesitation, "I am vexed at the
foolish thing you have done.   Not that it really
is at all a disgrace to you, or your family, but
that the world would take it so ; and we must
think as the world does."

"Must we ?" asked Hilary, smiling kindly ;
"well, if we must, let us think it on springs."

At the word he leaped into the fruit-van so
lightly that the strong springs scarcely shook ;
and Gregory could do no better than climb in
calmly after him. "Gee-wugg," cried Master
Shorne ; and he had no need to say it twice ;
the bright brass harness flashed in the sun, and
the horses merrily rang their hoofs, on the road
to their native land of Kent.

CHAPTER XIII.

TO THE CHERRY-ORCHARDS.

HILARY LORRAINE enjoyed his sudden delivery from London, and the fresh delight of the dewy country, with such loud approval, and such noisy lightsomeness of heart, that even Crusty John, perched high on the driving-box above him, could not help looking back now and then into the van, and affording the horses the benefit of his opinion. " A right down hearty one he be, as'll make some of our maids look alive. And the worst time of year for such work too, when the May-Dukes is in, and the Hearts a colouring!"

Hilary was sitting on an empty " half sieve," mounted on an empty bushel, and with his usual affability enjoying the converse of " Paddy from Cork," as everybody called the old Irishman, who served alike for farm, road, or market, as the "lad of all work." But Gregory Lovejoy, being of a somewhat grave and silent order, was already beginning to doubt his own prudence in bringing their impulsive friend so near to a certain fair cousin of his now staying at the hospitable farm, in whom he felt a tender interest. Poor Lovejoy feared that his chance would be small against this dashing stranger ; and he balanced uncomfortably in his mind, whether or not he should drop a hint, at the first opportunity, to Lorraine, concerning his views in that quarter. Often he almost resolved to do so ; and then to his diffidence it seemed presumptuous to fancy that any young fellow of Hilary's birth and expectations would entangle himself in their rustic world.

At Bromley they pulled up, to bait " man and beast," three fine horses and four good men, eager to know the reason why they should not have their breakfast. Lorraine, although very short of cash (as he always found the means to be), demanded and stood out for leave to pay for everybody. This privilege was obtained at last—as it generally is by persistency—and after that it was felt that Hilary could no longer be denied his manifest right to drive the van. He had driven the Brighton four-horse coach, the whole way to London, times and again ; and it was perfectly absurd to suppose that he could not manage three horses. Master John Shorne yielded his seat, apparently to this reasoning, but really to his own sure knowledge that the horses after so long a journey would be, on their way to stall, as quiet as lambs in the evening. Therefore he rolled himself up in the van, and slept the sleep of the man who has been up and wide-awake all night, for the sake of other people.

The horses well knew the true way home, and offered no cause for bit or whip; and they seemed to be taken sometimes with the pleasure which Hilary found in addressing them. They lifted their tails, and they pricked their ears, at the proper occasions genially; till the heat of the day settled down on their backs, and their creases grew dark and then lathery. And the horsefly (which generally forbears the pleasure of nuisance till July) in this unusually hot summer was earnest in his vocation already. Therefore, being of a leisurely mind, as behoves all genuine sons of the soil, Master Shorne called a halt, through the blazing time of noon, before battling with the " Backbone of Kent," as the beautiful North Down range is called. Here in a secluded glen they shunned the heats of Canicula under the sign of the " Pig and Whistle."

Thus the afternoon was wearing when they came to Sevenoaks, and passing through that pleasant town descended into the weald of Kent. No one but Hilary cared for the wonderful beauty and richness of the view, breadth upon breadth of fruitland, woven in and out with hops and corn ; and towards the windings of the Medway, pastures of the deepest green, even now after the heat of the sun, and thirst of the comet that drank the dew. Turning on the left from the Tunbridge road, they threaded their way along narrow lanes, where the hedges no longer were scarred with chalk, but tapestried with all shades of green, and even in the broken places, rich with little cascades of loam. Careless dogrose played above them with its loose abandonment ; and honeysuckle was almost ready to release its clustered tongues. But "Travellers' Joy"— the joy that makes all travellers long to rest in Kent—abode as yet in the hopeful bud, a pendent shower of emerald.

These things were not heeded much, but pleasantly accepted, by the four men and three horses. All felt alike that the world was made for them, and for them to enjoy themselves ; and little they cared to go into the reason,

when they had the room for it. With this large
sense of what ought to be, they came to the
gate of Old Applewood farm, a great white gate
with a padlock on it. This stopped the road,
and was meant to do so; for Martin Lovejoy,
Gregory's father, claimed the soil of the road
from this point, and denied all right of way,
public or even private, to all claimants of what-
soever kind. On the other hand the parish
claimed it as a public thoroughfare, and two
farmers further on vowed that it was an " occu-
pation road;" and what was more they would
use it as such. " Grower Lovejoy," as the
neighbourhood called him—not that he was
likely to grow much more, but because of his
cherry-orchards—here was the proper man to
hold the gate against all his enemies. When
they sawed it down, he very promptly replaced
it with cast-iron; and when this was shattered
with a fold-pitcher, he stopped their premature
triumph by a massive barrier of wrought metal
case-hardened against rasp or cold chisel.
Moreover he painted it white, so that any
nocturnal attack might be detected at a greater
distance.

When Paddy had opened this gate with a
key which he had carried to London, they

passed through an orchard of May-Duke cherries, with the ripe fruit hanging quite over the
road. "No wonder you lock the gate," said
Lorraine, as Crusty John, now on the box again,
handed him a noble cluster, with the dark juice
mantling richly under the ruddy gloss of skin.

"Do you mean that we should get them
stolen?" Gregory asked, with some indignation;
for his Kentish pride was touched: "oh, no, we
should never get them stolen. Nobody about
here would do such a thing."

"Then they don't know what's good," answered Hilary, jumping at another cluster; "I
was born to teach the Kentish public the proper
way to steal cherries."

"Well, they do take them sometimes," the
truthful Gregory confessed; "but we never call
it stealing, any more than we do what the birds
take."

"Valued fellow-student, thy strong point will
not be the criminal law. But you must have a
criminal love of the law, to jump at it out of
these cherry-trees."

"It was my mother's work, as you know.
Ah, there she is, and my Cousin Phyllis!"

For the moment Lovejoy forgot his duty
to his friend and particular guest, and slipping

down from the tail of the van, made off at full
speed through the cherry-trees. Hilary scarcely
knew what to do. The last thing that ever
occurred to him was that any one had been
rude to him; still it was rather unpleasant to
drive, or be driven, up to the door of his host,
sitting upon a bushel basket, and with no one
to say who he was. Yet to jump out and run
after Gregory, and collar him while he saluted
his mother, was even a worse alternative. In
a very few moments that chance was gone; for
the team, with the scent of their corn so nigh,
broke into a merry canter, and rattled along
with their ears pricked forward, and a pleasant
jingling. Neither did they stop until they
turned into a large farmyard, with an oast-house
at the further end of it. The dwelling-house
was of the oldest fashion, thatched in the middle,
at each end gabled, tiled in some places, and at
some parts slabbed. Yet, on the whole, it
looked snug, dry, and happy. Here, with one
accord, they halted, and shook themselves in
their harness, and answered the neighs of their
friends in the stables.

Hilary, laughing at his own plight, but feeling uncommonly stiff in the knees, arose from
his basket, and looked around; and almost the

first thing that met his gaze destroyed all his usual presence of mind. This was a glance of deep surprise, mingled with timid inquiry and doubt, from what Master Hilary felt at once to be the loveliest, sweetest, and most expressive brown eyes in the universe. The young girl blushed as she turned away, through fear of having shown curiosity; but the rich tint of her cheeks was faint, compared with the colour of poor Lorraine's. That gay youth was taken aback so utterly by the flash of a moment, that he could not find a word to say, but made pretence in a wholesale manner to see nothing at all particular. But the warm blood from his heart belied him, which he turned away to hide, and worked among the baskets briskly, hoping to be looked at, and preparing to have another look as soon as he felt that it could be done.

Meanwhile, that formidable creature, whose glance had produced such a fine effect, recovered more promptly from surprise, and felt perhaps the natural pride of success, and desire to pursue the fugitive. At any rate, she was quite ready to hear whatever he might have to say for himself.

· "I must ask you to forgive me," Lorraine began in a nervous manner, lifting his hat, and still blushing freely, "for springing so suddenly out of the earth—or rather, out of this van, I mean; though that can't be right, for I still am in it. I believe that I have the pleasure of speaking to Miss Phyllis Catherow. Your cousin, Mr. Lovejoy, is a very great friend of mine indeed; and he most kindly asked, or rather, what I mean to say is, invited me to come down for a day or two to this delightful part of the world; and I have enjoyed it so much already, that I am sure—that—that in fact——"

"That I hope you may soon enjoy it more." She did not in the least mean any sarcasm or allusion to Hilary's present state; still he fancied that she did; until the kind look, coming so sweetly from the kind warm heart, convinced him that she never could be so cruel.

"I see the most delightful prospect I ever could imagine of enjoying myself," Lorraine replied, with a glance, imparting to his harmless words the mischief of that which nowadays we call "a most unwarrantable personal allusion." But she did not, or would not, take it so.

"How kind of you to be pleased so lightly! But we do our best, in our simple way, when any one kindly comes to see us."

"Why, Miss Catherow, I thought from what your cousin said to me that you were only staying here for a little time yourself." ·

"You are quite right as to Miss Catherow. But I am not my Cousin Phyllis. I am only Mabel Lovejoy, Gregory Lovejoy's sister."

"By Jove, how glad I am!" cried Hilary, in his impetuous way; "what a fool I must have been not to know it, after I saw him run to meet his cousin in the orchard! But that treacherous Gregory never told me that he ever had a sister. Now, won't I thoroughly give it to him?"

"You must not be angry, Mr. Lorraine, with poor Gregory, because—because Phyllis is such a beautiful girl."

"Don't let me hear about beautiful girls! As if—as if there could be any——"

"Good enough for Gregory," she answered, coming cleverly to his rescue, for he knew that he had gone too far; "but wait till you have seen Cousin Phyllis."

"There is one thing I shall not defer for the glory of seeing a thousand Miss Catherows, and that is the right that I have to shake hands with my dear friend Gregory's sister."

He had leaped from the van some time ago,

and now held out his hand (a good strong one, pleasingly veined with cherry-juice), and she, with hospitable readiness, laid her pretty palm therein. He felt that it was a pretty hand, and a soft one, and a hearty one ; and he found excuse to hold it longer, while he asked a question.

" Now, how did you know my name, if you please, while I made such a stupid mistake about yours ? "

" By your bright blue eyes," she was going to answer, with her native truthfulness ; but the gaze of those eyes suggested that the downright truth might be dangerous. Therefore, for once, she met a question with a question warily.

" Was it likely that I should not know you, after all I have heard of you ? " This pleased him well in a general way. For Hilary, though too free (if possible) from conceit and arrogance, had his own little share of vanity. Therefore, upon the whole, it was lucky, and showed due attention to his business, that Grower Lovejoy now came up, to know what was doing about the van.

Martin Lovejoy was not a squatter, by seven years stamped into "tenant right," which means for the most part landlord's wrong. Nor was he one of those great tenant farmers who, even then, were beginning to rise, and hold their own with "landed gentry." His farm was small, when compared with some; but it was outright his own, having descended to him through long-buried generations. So that he was one of the ever-dwindling class of "franklins," a class that has done good work for England, neither obtaining nor wanting thanks.

Old Applewood farm contained altogether about six hundred acres, whereof at least two-thirds lay sweetly in the Vale of Medway, and could show root, stem, or bine against any other land in Kent, and therefore any in England. Here was no fear of the heat of the sun, or the furious winter's rages, such a depth of nature underlay the roots of everything. Nothing ever suffered from that poverty of blood which makes trees canker on a shallow soil; and no tree rushed into watery strength (which very soon turns to weakness), through having laid hold upon something that suited only a particular part of it.

And not the trees alone, but all things, grew within that proper usage of a regulated power (yet with more of strength to come up, if it should be called for), which has made our land and country fertile over all the world; receiving submissively the manners and the manure of all nations.   This is a thing to be proud of; but the opportunity for such pride was not open to the British mind at the poor old time now dealt with.

Martin Lovejoy knew no more than that the rest of Europe was amassed against our island; and if England meant to be England, every son of that old country must either fight himself or pay.   Martin would rather have fought than paid, if he had only happened to be a score and a half years younger.

Hilary Lorraine knew well (when Martin Lovejoy took his hand, and welcomed him to Old Applewood) that here was a man to be relied on, to make good his words and mind. A man of moderate stature, but of sturdy frame, and some dignity; ready to meet every-body pretty much as he was met.

"Glad to see you, sir," he said; "I have often heard of you, Master Lorraine; it is right kind of you to come down.   I hope that you are really hungry, sir."

" To the last degree," answered Hilary;

"I have been eating off and on, but nothing at all to speak of, in the noble air I have travelled through."

"Our air has suited you, I see by the colour of your cheeks and eyes.   Aha! the difference begins, as I have seen some scores of times, at ten miles out of London.   And we are nearly thirty here, sir, from that miserable place.   Excuse me, Master Lorraine, I hope I say nothing to offend you."

"My dear sir, how can you offend me?   I hate London heartily.   There must be a million people there a great deal too good to live in it. We are counting everybody this year; and I hear that when it is made up there will be a million and a quarter!"

"I can't believe it.   I cannot believe it. There never was such a deal before.   And how can there want to be so many now?   This numbering of the people is an unholy thing, that leads to plagues.   All the parsons around here say that this has brought the comet.   And they may show something for it; and they preach of Jerusalem when it was going to be destroyed.   They have frightened all our young maids terribly.   What is said in London, sir?"

"Scarcely anything, Mr. Lovejoy: scarcely

anything at all. We only see him every now and then, because of the smoke between us. And when we see him, we have always got our own work to attend to."

"Wonderful, wonderful!" answered the Grower; "who can make out them Londoners? About their business they would go if Korah, Dathan, and Abiram were all swallowed up in front of them. For that I like them. I like a man—but come in to our little supper, sir."

CHAPTER XIV.

BEAUTIES OF THE COUNTRY.

THE next day was Sunday; and Hilary (having brought a small bag of clothes with him) spent a good deal of the early time in attending to his adornment. For this he had many good reasons to give, if only he had thought about them; but the only self-examination that occurred to him was at the looking-glass. Here he beheld himself looking clean and bright, as he always did look; and yet he was not quite satisfied (as he ought to have been) with his countenance. "There is room for a lot of improvement," he exclaimed at himself, quite bitterly: "how coarse, and how low, I begin to look! But there is not a line in her face that could be changed without spoiling it. There again! Hairs, hairs, coming almost everywhere! Beautiful girls have none of that stuff. How they must despise us! All their hair is ornamental, and ours comes so disgracefully!"

When he had no one else to talk to, Hilary always talked to himself. He always believed that he knew himself better than anybody else could know him. And so he had a right to do; and so he must have done just now, if doubtful watch of himself and great shaking of his head could help him.

At last he began to be fit to go down, according to his own ideas, though not at all sure that he might not have managed to touch himself up just a little bit more—which might make all the difference. He thought that he looked pretty well; but still he would have liked to ask Gregory before it was too late to make any change, and the beautiful eyes fell upon him. But Gregory, and all the rest, were waiting for him in the breakfast-room; and no one allowed him to suspect how much he had tried their patience.

Young Lovejoy showed a great deal of skill in keeping Lorraine to the other side of the table from Phyllis Catherow; and Hilary was well content to sit at the side of Mabel. Phyllis, in his opinion, was a beautiful girl enough, and clever in her way, and lively; but "lovely" was the only word to be used at all about Mabel. And she asked him to have just a spoonful of honey, and to share a pat of butter with her, in such a voice, and with such a look, that if she had said, "here are two ounces of cold-drawn castor oil—if you take one, I'll take the other," he must have opened his mouth for it.

So they went on; and neither knew the deadly sin they were dropping to—that deadly sin of loving when the level and entire landscape of two lives are different.

Through the rich fields, and across a pretty little wandering brook, which had no right to make a quarter of the noise it was making, this snug party went to church. Accurate knowledge of what to do, as well as very pretty manners, and a sound resolve to be over-nice (rather than incur the possibility of pushing), led the two young men from London rather to underdo the stiles, and almost go quite away, than to express their feelings by hands, whenever the top-bar made a tangle, according to the usual knot of it. The two girls entered into this, and said to themselves, what a very superior thing it was to have young men from London, in comparison with young hop-growers, who

stood here and there across them, and made
them so blush for each inch of their legs.
What made it all the more delicate, and ever
so much more delightful, was, that the excellent
Grower was out of the way, and so was Mrs.
Lovejoy. For the latter, being a most kind-
hearted woman, had rheumatic pains at the first
church-bell, all up the leaders of her back; so
that the stiles were too many for her, and
Master Lovejoy was compelled to drive her
in the one-horse shay.

By the time these staid young men and
maidens came to the little churchyard gate,
everything was settled between them, as if by
deed under hand and seal, although not so
much as a wave of the air, much less any
positive whisper of the wind, had stirred therein.
The import of this unspoken and even un-
dreamed covenant was, that Gregory now must
walk with Phyllis, and see to her, and look at
her, without her having any second thoughts
concerning Hilary. Hilary, on the other hand,
was to be acknowledged as the cavalier of
Mabel; to help her when she wanted helping,
and to talk when she wanted talking; although
it night be assumed quite fairly that she could
do most of that for herself. Feeling the

strength of good management, all of them marched into church accordingly.

In the very same manner they all marched out, after behaving uncommonly well, and scarcely looking at one another, when the clergyman gave out that the heat of the weather had not allowed him to write a new discourse that week ; but as the same cause must have made them forgetful of what he had said last Sunday (when many of them seemed inattentive), he now proposed, with the Divine assistance, to read the same sermon again to them.

With the unconverted youthful mind, a spring (like that of Jack-out-of-the-box) at the outer door of the church jumps up, after being so long inside, into that liberal good-will, which is one of our noblest sentiments. Anybody is glad to see almost everybody ; and people (though of one parish) in great joy forego their jangling. The sense of a grand relief, and a conscience wiped clean for another week, leads the whole lot to love one another as far as the gate of the churchyard.

But our young people were much inclined to love one another much further. The more they got into the meadow-land, and the strength of the summer around them, with the sharp stroke of the sun, and the brisk short shadows of one another, the more they were treading a dangerous path, and melting away to each other. Hilary saw with romantic pride that Mabel went on as well as ever, and had not a bead on her clear bright cheeks; while at the same time Phyllis, though stopping to rest every now and then—but. Hilary never should have noticed this. Such things are below contempt.

In this old and genial house, the law was that the guest should appoint the time for dinner, whenever the cares of the outer work permitted it. And as there were no such cares on Sunday, Hilary had to choose the time for the greatest event of the human day. This had been talked of and settled, of course, before anybody got the prayer-books; and now the result at two o'clock was a highly excellent repast. To escape the power of the sun they observed this festival in the hall of the house, which was deliciously cool even now, being paved with stone, and shaded by a noble and fragrant walnut-tree. Mrs. Lovejoy knew, what many even good housekeepers seem not to know —to wit that, to keep a room cool, it is not

necessary to open the windows when the me-
ridian sun bombards. " For goodness' sake, let
us have some air in such weather as this!" they
cry, when they might as well say, "let us cool
the kitchen by opening the door of the oven."

Lorraine was one of those clever fellows who
make the best of everything ; which is the
cleverest thing that can be done by a human
being. And he was not yet come to the time
of life when nothing is good if the dinner is
bad ; so that he sat down cheerily, and cheered
all the rest by doing so.

Of course there were many things said and
done, which never would have been said, or
thought of, at the dinner-table of Coombe
Lorraine. But Hilary (though of a very sensitive fibre in such matters) neither saw, nor
heard, nor felt, a single thing that irked him.
There was nothing low about anybody ; whereas there was something as high as the heavens
dining out of the very next plate. He made
himself (to the very utmost of his power) agreeable, except at the moments when his power of
pleasing quite outran himself. Then he would
stop and look at his fork—one of the fine old
two-pronged fellows—and almost be afraid to
glance, to ask what she was thinking.

She was thinking the very things that she should have known better than to think. But what harm could there possibly be in scarcely thinking, so much as dreaming, things that could have nothing in them? Who was she, a country-girl, to set herself up, and behave herself, as if anybody meant anything? And yet his eyes, and the bend of his head, and his choice of that kidney-potato for her (as if he were born a grower)—and then the way he poured her beer—if there was nothing in all this, why then there was nothing in all the world, except delusion and breaking of heart.

Hilary, sitting at her knife-hand, felt a whole course of the like emotions, making allowance for gender. How beautifully she played her knife, with a feminine tenderness not to make a cruel slice of anything! And how round her little wrist was, popping in and out of sleeves, according as the elbow went; and no knob anywhere to be seen, such as women even of the very latest fashion have. And then her hair was coming towards him (when she got a bit of gristle) so that he could take a handful, if the other people only would have the manners not to look. And oh, what lovely hair it was! so silky, and so rich, and bright,

and full of merry dances to the music of her
laugh! And he did not think he had ever seen
anything better than her style of eating, without showing it. Clearly enjoying her bit of
food, and tempting all to feed their best; yet
full of mind at every mouthful, and of heart at
every help. But above all, when she looked
up, quite forgetting both knife and fork, and
looked as if she could look like that into no
other eyes but his; with such a gentle flutter,
and a timid wish to tell no more, and yet a
sudden pulse of glad light from the innocent
young heart—nothing could be lovelier than
the way in which she raised her eyes, except
her way of dropping them.

These precious glances grew more rare and
brief the more he sought for them; and he
wondered whether anybody else ever had been
treated so. Then, when he would seem to be
doubtful, and too much inclined to stop, a look
of surprise, or a turn of the head, would tempt
him to go on again. And there would be little
moments (both on his side and on hers) of
looking about at other people with a stealthy
richness: With a sense of some great treasure,
made between them, and belonging to themselves in private; a proud demand that the

rest of the world should attend to its proper
business ; and then, with one accord, a meeting
of the eyes that were beginning, more and more,
to mean alike.

All this was as nice as could be, and a pretty
thing to see.   Still, in a world that always
leaves its loftiest principles to accumulate, at
the lowest interest (and once in every generation to be a mere drug in the market), "love"
is used, not in games alone, as the briefest form
of "nothing."   All our lovers (bred as lovers
must be under school boards) know what they
are after now, and who can pay the ninepence.
But in the ancient time, the mothers had to see
to most of that.

Mrs. Lovejoy, though she did not speak, or
look particularly, had her perception of what
was going on close by.   And she said to herself, " I will see to this.   It is no good inter-
fering now.   I shall have Miss Mabel all to
myself in three-quarters of an hour."

CHAPTER XV.

MRS. LOVEJOY'S lecture to her daughter seemed likely to come just a little too late, as so many excellent lessons do. For as soon as he saw that all had dined, the host proposed an adjournment, which was welcomed with no small delight by all except the hostess.

"Now, Master Lorraine, and my niece Phyllis, what say you, if we gather our fruit for ourselves in the shady places; or rather, if we sit on the bank of the little brook in the orchard, where there is a nice sheltered spot; and there we can have a glass of wine while the maidens pick the fruit for us?"

"Capital," answered Hilary; "what a fine idea, Mr. Lovejoy! But surely we ought to pick for the ladies, instead of letting them pick for us."

" No, sir, we will let them have the pleasure of waiting upon us. It is the rule of this neighbourhood, and ought to be observed everywhere. We work for the ladies all the week, serve, honour, and obey them. On Sundays they do the like for us, and it is a very pleasant change. Mabel, don't forget the pipes. Do you smoke, Master Lorraine? If so, my daughter will fill a pipe for you."

" That would be enough to tempt me, even if I disliked it, whereas I am very fond of it. However, I never do smoke, because my father has a most inveterate prejudice against it. I promised him some time ago to give it up for a twelvemonth. And the beauty of it is that there is nothing he himself enjoys so much as a good pinch of snuff. Ah, there I am getting my revenge upon him. My sister will do any-thing I ask her; and he will do anything she asks him : and so, without his knowledge, I am breaking him of his snuff-box."

" Aha, well done! I like that. And I like you too, young man, for your obedience to your father. That virtue is becoming very rare; rarer and rarer every year. Why, if my father had knocked me down I should have lain on the ground, if it was a nettle-bed, till he told me to get up. Now, Greg, my boy, what would you do ? "

" Well, sir, I think that I should get up as quick as I could, and tell my mother."

" Aha! and I should have the nettles then. Well said, Greg, my boy ; I believe it is what all the young fellows nowadays would do. But I don't mean you, of course, Master Lorraine. Come along, come along. Mabel, you know where that old Madeira is that your poor Uncle Ambrose took three times to Calcutta. Ah, poor man, I wish he was here! As fine a fellow as ever shotted a cannon at a French-man. Nelson could have done no better. And it did seem uncommonly hard upon him never to go to churchyard. However, the will of the Lord be done! Now mind, the new patent cork-screw."

Mabel was only too glad to get this errand to the cellar. With filial instinct she perceived how likely she was to " catch it," as soon as her mother got the chance. Not that she deserved it. Oh no, not in the least, her conscience told her. Was she to be actually rude to her father's guest, and her brother's friend ? And as if she was not old enough now, at eighteen and a quarter, to judge for herself in such

childish matters as how to behave at dinner-
time !

By the side of a pebbly brook—which ran
within stone-throw of the house, sparkling fresh
and abundant from ·deep well-springs of the
hill-range—they came to a place which seemed
to be made especially for enjoyment : a bend
of the grassy banks and rounded hollow of the
fruit-land, where cherry, and apple, and willow-
tree clubbed their hospitable shade, and fugitive
water made much ado to ripple down the zigzag
rill.   Here in cool and gentle shelter, the Grower
set his four legs down ; *i.e.*, the four legs of his
chair, because, like all that in gardens dwell,
he found mother earth too rheumatic for him,
especially in hot weather when deep sluggish
fibres radiate.   The Groweress also had her
chair, borne by the sedulous Hilary.   All the
rest, like nymphs and shepherds, strewed their
recumbent forms on turf.

"God Almighty," said Master Lovejoy, fearing that he might be taking it too easy for the
Sabbath-day, "really hath made beautiful things
for us His creatures to rejoice in, with praise,
thanksgiving, and fruitfulness.   Mabel, put them
two bottles in the brook—not there, you stupid
child ; can't you see that the sun comes under

that old root ? In the corner where that shelf
of stone is.   Thank you, Master Lorraine.
What a thing it is to have a headpiece ! But
God Almighty never made, among all His
wonderful infinite works, the waters and the
great whales, and the fruit-tree yielding fruit,
whose seed is in itself, and the green herb for
meat, which means to come to table with the
meat ; His mercy endureth for ever ; and He
never showed it as when He made tobacco,
and clay for tobacco-pipes—the white clay that
He made man of."   With this thanksgiving he
began to smoke.

"Now, Martin, I never could see that," answered Mrs. Lovejoy ; "the best and greatest
work of the Lord ought to have been for the
women first."

"Good wife, then it must have been the
apple.   Ah, Gregory, I had your mother there !
However, we won't dispute on a Sunday ; it
spoils all the goodness of going to church, and
never leaves anything settled.   Mabel, run
away now for the fruit, while Gregory feels if
the wine is cold.   Master Lorraine, I hope our
little way of going on, and being over free on a
Sunday perhaps, does not come amiss to you."

Hilary did not look as if anything came

amiss to him, as now he lay at the feet of
Mabel, on the slope of the sweet rich sward,
listening only for her voice, more liquid than
even the tone of the brook. He listened for
it, but not to it; inasmuch as one of those
sudden changes, which (at less than half a
breath) vapour the glass of the feminine mind,
was having its turn with the maiden. Mabel
felt that she had not kept herself to herself, as
she should have done. Who was this gentleman, or what, that she should be taken with
him so suddenly as to feel her breath come
short, every time that she even thought of
her mother? A gentleman from London too,
where the whole time of the Court was spent,
as Master Shorne brought news every week,
in things that only the married women were
allowed to hear of. In the present case, of
course, she knew how utterly different all things
were. How lofty and how grand of heart, how
fearful even to look at her much—still, for all
that, it would only be wise to show him, or at
least to let him see that—that at any rate, for
the present——

"Now, Mabel, when are you going for the
cherries? Phyllis — bless my heart alive!
Gregory, are you gone to sleep? What are

all the young people made of, when a touch of summer shows them only fit to sprawl about?"

"Bring three sorts of cherries, Mabel," Gregory shouted after her; "Mr. Lorraine must be tired of May-Dukes, I am sure. The Black Geans must be ripe, and the Eltons, and the Early Amber. And go and see how the White-hearts are on the old tree against the wall."

"Much he knows about cherries, I believe!" grumbled Mr. Lovejoy; "John Doe and Richard Roe be more to his liking than the finest Griffins. Why, the White-hearts haven't done stoning yet! What can the boy be thinking of?" It was the Grower's leading grievance that neither of his two sons seemed likely to take to the business after him. Here was the elder being turned by his mother into a "thieves' counsellor," and the younger was away at sea, and whenever he came home told stories of foreign fruit which drove his father into a perfect fury. So that now it was Martin's main desire to marry his only daughter to some one fitted to succeed him, who might rent the estate from Gregory the heir; for the land had been disgavelled.

It is a pleasing thing to a young man—ay,

and an old one may be pleased—to see a pretty
girl make herself useful in pretty and natural
attitudes; and that pleasure now might be
enjoyed at leisure and in duplicate.   For
Phyllis Catherow was a pretty, or rather a
beautiful young woman, slender, tall, and fair
of hue.   Not to be compared with Mabel,
according to Hilary's judgment; but infinitely
superior to her, in the opinion of Gregory.   All
that depends upon taste, of course; but Mabel's
beauty was more likely to outlast the flush of
youth, having the keeping qualities of a bright
and sweet expression, and the kind lustre of
sensible eyes.

These two went among the cherry-trees, with
fair knowledge what to do, and having light
scarves on their heads, brought behind their
ears and tied under the curves of their single
chins.   Because they knew that the spurs and
sprays would spoil their lovely Sunday hats,
even without the drip of a cherry wounded
by some thirsty thrush.   The blackbirds pop
them off entire, and so do the starlings;
but the thrushes sit and peck at them, with
the juice dripping down on their dappled
breasts, and a flavour in their throats, which
they mean to sing about at their leisure.   But

now the birds, that were come among them, meant to have them wholesale. Phyllis, being a trifle taller, and less deft of finger, bent the shady branches down, for Mabel to pluck the fruit. Mabel knew that she must take the northern side of the tree, of course; and the boughs where the hot sun had not beaten through the leaves and warmed the fruit. Also she knew that she must not touch the fruit with her hand and dim the gloss; but above all things to be careful—as of the goose with the golden eggs—to make no havoc of the young buds forming, at the base of every cluster, for the promise of next year's crop.

Hilary longed to go and help them; but his host being very proud of the grandeur of his Madeira wine, would not even hear of it. And Mrs. Lovejoy, for other reasons, showed much skill in holding him; so that he could but sit down and admire the picture he longed to be part of. Hence he beheld, in the happy distance, in and out the well-fed trees, skill, and grace, and sprightly movements, tiny baskets lifted high, round arms bent for drawing downward, or thrown up for a jumping catch, and everything else that is so lovely, and safe to admire at a distance.

By-and-by the maids came back, bearing their juicy treasure, and blithe with some sage mysticism of laughter. They had hit upon some joke between them, or something that chanced to tickle them; and when this happens with girls, they never seem to know when the humour is out of it; and of course they make the deepest mystery of a diminutive jest so harmless that it hits no one except themselves. Mrs. Lovejoy looked at them strongly. Her time for common-sense was come; and she thought they were stealing a march upon her, by some whispers about young men, the last thing they should ever think of.

Whereas the poor girls had no thought of anything of the kind. Neither would they think one atom more than they could help, of what did not in the least concern them; if their elders, who laid down the law, would only leave them to themselves. And it was not long till this delightful discretion was afforded them. For, after a glass or two of wine, the heat of the day began to tell, through the cool air of the hollow, on that worthy couple, now kindly hand in hand, and calmly going down the slope of life. They hoped they had got a long way to go yet; and each thought so of the other.

Neither of them had much age, being well under threescore years; just old enough to begin to look on the generation judiciously. But having attained this right at last, after paying heavily, what good could they have of it, if young people were ever so far beyond their judgment? Meditating thus they dozed; and youthful voice, and glance, and smile, were drowned in the melody of—nose.

The breeze that comes in the afternoon of every hot day (unless the sky is hushing up for a thunderstorm) began to show the underside of leaves and the upper gloss of grass, and with feeble puffs to stir the stagnant heat into vibration, like a candle quivering. Every breath at first was hot, and only made the air feel hotter, until there arrived a refreshing current, whether from some water-meadows, or from the hills where the chalk lay cool.

"The heat is gone," said Martin Lovejoy, waking into the pleasant change; "it will be a glorious afternoon. Pooh, what is this to call hot weather? Only three years ago, in 1808, I remember well——"

"It may have been hotter then, my dear," said Mrs. Lovejoy, placidly; "but it did not make you forget your pipe, and be ungrateful to Providence about me."

"Why, where can the children be?" cried the Grower. "I thought they were all here just this moment! It is wonderful how they get away together. I thought young Lorraine and Gregory were as fast asleep as you or I! Oh, there, I hear them in the distance, with the girls, no doubt, all alive and merry!"

"Ay, and a little too merry, I doubt," answered Mrs. Lovejoy; "a little too much alive for me. Why, they must be in the wall-garden now! Goodness, alive, I believe they are, and nobody to look after them!"

"Well, if they are, they can't do much harm. They are welcome to anything they can find, except the six strawberries I crossed, and Mabel will see that they don't eat those."

"Crossed strawberries indeed! now, Martin," Mrs. Lovejoy never could be brought to understand cross-breeding; "they'll do something worse than cross your strawberries, unless you keep a little sharper look-out. They'll cross your plans, Master Martin Lovejoy, and it's bad luck for any one who does that."

"I don't understand you, wife, any more than you understand the strawberries. How could they cross them at this time of year?"

"Why, don't you see that this gay young

Lorraine is falling over head and ears in love with our darling Mabel?"

"Whew! That would be a sad affair," the Grower answered carelessly: "I like the young fellow, and should be sorry to have him so disappointed. For of course he never could have our Mab, unless he made up his mind to turn grower. Shorne says that he is a born salesman; perhaps he is also a born grower."

"Now, husband, why do you vex me so? You know as well as I do that he is the only son of a baronet, belonging, as Gregory says, to one of the proudest families in England; though he doesn't show much pride himself, that's certain. Is it likely they would let him have Mabel?"

"Is it likely that we would let Mabel have him? But this is all nonsense, wife; you are always discovering such mare's-nests. Tush! why, I didn't fall in love with you till we fell off a horse three times together."

"I know that, of course. But that was because they wanted us to do it. The very thing is that it happens at once when everybody's face is against it. However, you've had your warning, Martin, and you only laugh at it. You have nobody but yourself to thank, if it goes against your plots and plans. For my own part, I should be well pleased if Mabel were really fond of him, and if the great people came round in the end, as sooner or later they always do. There are very few families in the kingdom that need be ashamed of my daughter, I think. And he is a most highly accomplished young man. He said last night immediately after prayer-time that I might try for an hour, and he would be most happy to listen to me, but I never, never could persuade him that I was over forty years old. Therefore, husband, see to it yourself. Things may take their own course for me."

"Trust me, trust me, good wife," said Martin; "I can see, as far as most folk can. What stupes boys and girls are, to be sure, to go rushing about after watery fruit, and leave such wine as this here Madeira. Have another glass, my dear good creature, to cheer you up after your prophecies."

Meanwhile, in the large old-fashioned garden, which lay at the east end of the house, further up the course of the brook, any one sitting among the currant-bushes might have judged which of the two was right, the unromantic franklin, or his more ambitious but sensible wife. Gregory and Phyllis were sitting quietly in a

fine old arbour, having a steady little flirt of
their own, and attending to nothing in the
world besides.   Phyllis was often of a pensive
cast, and she never looked better than in this
mood, when she felt the deepest need of sympathy.   This she was receiving now, and pretending of course not to care for it ; her fingers
played with moss and bark, the fruits of the
earth were below her contempt, and she looked
too divine for anybody.

On the other hand, the rarest work and the
most tantalizing tricks were going on, at a proper distance, between young Mabel and Hilary.
They had straggled off into the strawberry-beds,
where nobody could see them ; and there they
seemed likely to spend some hours if nobody
should come after them.   The plants were of the
true Carolina, otherwise called the " old scarlet
pine," which among all our countless new sorts
finds no superior, perhaps no equal; although it is
now quite out of vogue, because it fruits so shyly.

What says our chief authority ? *   " Fruit
medium-sized, ovate, even, and regular, and
with a glossy neck, skin deep red, flesh pale
red, very firm and solid, with a fine sprightly
and very rich pine flavour."   What lovelier

* That admirable writer, Dr. Hogg.

fruit could a youth desire to place between little
pearly teeth, reserving the right to have a bite,
if any of the very firm flesh should be left ?
'What fruit more suggestive of elegant compli-
ments could a maid open her lips to receive,
with a dimple in each mantled cheek—lips more
bright than the skin of the fruit, cheeks by no
means of a pale red now, although very firm
and solid—and as for the sprightly flavour of
the whole, it may be imagined, if you please,
but is not to be ascertained as yet ?

" Now, I must pick a few for you, Mr.
Lorraine. You are really giving me all you
find. And they are so scarce—no, thank you ;
I can get up very nicely by myself. And there
can't be any brier in my hair. You really do
imagine things, Where on earth could it have
come from ? . Well, if you are sure, of course
you may remove it. Now I verily believe you
put it there. Well, perhaps I am wronging you.
It was an unfair thing to say, I confess. Now
wait a moment, while I run to get a little
cabbage-leaf ! "

" A cabbage leaf ! Now you are too bad. I
won't taste so much as the tip of a strawberry
out of anything but one. How did you eat
your strawberries, pray ? "

"With my mouth, of course. But explain your meaning. You won't eat what I pick for you out of what?"

"Out of anything else in the world except your own little beautiful palm."

"Now, how very absurd you are! Why, my hands are quite hot."

"Let me feel them and judge for myself. Now the other, if you please. Oh, how lovely and cool they are! How could you tell me such a story, Mabel, beautiful Mabel?"

"I am not at all beautiful, and I won't be called so. And I know not what they may do in London. But I really think, considering—at least when one comes to consider that——"

"To consider what? You make me tremble, you do look so ferocious. Ah, I thought you couldn't do it long. Inconsiderate creature, what is it I am to consider?"

"You cannot consider! Well, then, remember. Remember, it is not twenty-four hours since you saw me for the very first time; and surely it is not right and proper that you should begin to call me 'Mabel,' as if you had known me all your life!"

"I must have known you all my life. And

I mean to know you all the rest of my life, and
a great deal more than that——"

"It may be because you are Gregory's
friend you are allowed to do things. But what
would you think of me, Mr. Lorraine, if I were
to call you 'Hilary'—a thing I should never
dream of ?"

"I should think that you were the very kindest darling, and I should ask you to breathe it
quite into my ear—' Hilary, Hilary !'—just like
that ; and then I should answer just like this,
' Mabel, Mabel, sweetest Mabel, how I love
you, Mabel !' and then what would you say, if
you please ? "

"I should have to ask my mother," said the
maiden, "what I ought to say. But luckily the
whole of this is in your imagination. Mr.
Lorraine, you have lost your strawberries by
your imagination."

"What do I care for strawberries ?" Hilary
cried, as the quick girl wisely beat a swift re-
treat from him. "You never can enter into
my feelings, or you never would run away like
that. And I can't run after you, you know,
because of Phyllis and Gregory. There she
goes, and she won't come back. What a fool I
was to be in such a hurry ! But what could I

do to help it? I never know where I am when she turns those deep rich eyes upon me. She never will show them again, I suppose, but keep the black lashes over them. And I was getting on so well—and here are the stalks of the strawberries!"

Of every strawberry she had eaten from his daring fingers he had kept the stalk and calyx, breathed on by her freshly fragrant breath, and slyly laid them in his pocket; and now he fell to at kissing them. Then he lay down in the Carolinas, where her skirt had moved the leaves; and to him, weary with strong heat, and a rush of new emotions, comfort came in the form of sleep. And when he awoke, in his open palm most delicately laid he found a little shell-shaped cabbage-leaf piled with the fruit of the glossy neck.

CHAPTER XVI.

OH, SWEETER THAN THE BERRY!

THESE doings of Hilary and his love—for his love he declared her to be for ever, whether she would have him for hers or not—seem to have taken more time almost in telling than in befalling. Although it had been a long summer's day, to them it had passed as a rapid dream. So at least they fancied, when they began to look quietly back at it, forgetting the tale of the golden steps so lightly flitted over by the winged feet of love.

Martin Lovejoy watched his daughter at supper-time that Sunday; and he felt quite sure that his wife was wrong. Why, the girl scarcely spoke to Lorraine at all, and even neglected his plate so sadly, that her mother was compelled to remind her sharply of her duties. Upon which the Grower despatched to his wife a smile of extreme sagacity, which (being fetched out of cipher and shorthand, by the matrimonial key) contained all this,—"Well, you are a silly, as you always are, when you want to advise me. The girl is cold-shouldering that young fellow, the same as she does all the young hop-growers. And well she knows how to do it too. She gets her intellect from her father. Now please not to put in your oar, Mrs. Lovejoy, another time, till it is asked for."

Moreover, he thought that if Mabel took the smallest delight in Hilary, she could not have answered as she had done, when that pious youth, in the early evening, expressed his sincere desire to attend another performance of Divine service.

"I had no idea," said the simple Gregory, "that you made a point of going to church at least twice every Sunday. I seldom see you of a Sunday in London. But the very last place I should go to, to find you, would probably be the Temple church."

"That is quite a different thing, don't you see? A country church, and a church in London, are as different as a meadow and a market-place."

"But surely, Mr. Lorraine, you would find the duty of attending just the same." Thus spoke

Mrs. Lovejoy, who seldom missed a chance of discharging her duty towards young people.

"Quite so, of course I do, Mrs. Lovejoy. But then we always perform our duties best, when they are pleasures. And besides that, I have a special reason for feeling bound, as one might say, to go to church well in the country."

"I suppose one must not venture to ask you what that reason is, sir."

"Oh, yes, to be sure. It is just this. I have an uncle, my mother's brother, who is a country clergyman."

"Well done, Master Lorraine!" said the Grower, while the rest were laughing. "You take a very sensible view, sir, of things. It is too much the fashion nowadays to neglect our trade-connections. But Gregory will go with you, and Phyllis, and Mabel. The old people stay at home to mind the house. For we always let the maid-servants go."

"Oh father," cried Mabel; "poor Phyllis is so overcome by the heat, that she must not go. And I must stop at home to read to her."

So that the good Lorraine took nothing by his sudden religious fervour, except a hot walk with Gregory, and a wearisome doze in a musty pew, with nobody to look at.

With fruit-growers, Monday is generally the busiest day of the week, except Friday. After paying all hands on the Saturday night, and stowing away all implements, they rest them well till the Sunday is over, having in the summer-time earned their rest, by night-work as well as day-work, through the weary hours of the week. This is not the case with all, of course. Many of them, especially down in Kent, grow their fruit, or let it grow itself, and then sell it by the acre, or the hundred acres, to dealers, who take all the gathering and marketing off their hands altogether. But for those who work off their own crops, the toil of the week begins before the daystar of the Monday. At least for about six weeks it is so, according to the weather and the length of the " busy season." Before the stars fade out of the sky, the pickers advance through the straw-berry quarters, carrying two punnets each, yawning more than chattering even, whisking the grey dew away with their feet, startling the lark from his nest in the row, groping among the crisp leaves for the fruit, and often laying hold of a slug instead.

That is the time for the true fruit-lover to try the taste of a strawberry. It should be one

that refused to ripen in the gross heat of yesterday, but has been slowly fostering 'goodness,
with the attestation of the stars. And now (if
it has been properly managed, properly picked
without touch of hand, and not laid down pro-
fanely), when the sun comes over the top of
the hedge, the look of that strawberry will be
this—at least, if it is of a proper sort. The
beard of the footstalk will be stiff, the sepals of
the calyx moist and crisp, the neck will show a
narrow band of varnish, where the dew could
find no hold, the belly of the fruit will be sleek
and gentle, firm however to accept its fate; but
the back that has dealt with the dew, and the
sides where the colour of the back slopes downward, upon them such a gloss of cold and
diamond chastity will lie, that the human lips
get out of patience with the eyes in no time.

Everybody was so busy with the way the
work went on, all for their very life pretending
scarcely to have time to breathe, whenever the
master looked at them, that the " berries " were
picked, and packed, and started, long before the
sun grew hot, started on the road to London,
the cormorant of the universe.

Hilary helped with all his heart; enjoying
it, with that triumphant entrance into any

novelty, which always truly distinguished him. He carried his punnets, and kept his row, (as soon as they had shown him how) as well as the very best of them, dividing his fruit into firsts, and seconds, and keeping the "toppers" separate. Of course he broke off many trusses entire — ripe fruit, green fruit, and barren blossom—until he learned how to "meet his nails," and how much drag to put on the stalks. A clever fellow learns all that from an hour or two of practice.

But one thing there is which the cleverest fellows can learn by no experience—how to carry the head for hours upside down without hurting it. How to make the brain so hard that it cannot shift; or else so soft that the top is as good as the bottom. The question is one for a great physician; who, to understand it, must keep his row, and pick by the job. Then let him say if he has learned how to explain the well-established fact that a woman can pick twice as fast as a man; for who could assent to the reason assigned by one of themselves mag-nanimously—that "they was generally always used to keep their heads turned upside down?"

Leaving such speculative inquiries to go on for ever, Hilary (who knew better than to say a

word about them) came in for his breakfast at
six o'clock, and ate it as thoroughly as he had
earned it. The master, a man of true Kentish
fibre, obstinate, placable, hearty, and dry, made
known to his wife and to everybody else, his
present opinion of Hilary. Martin Lovejoy
never swore. He never went beyond "God
knows," or "The Lord in heaven look down on
us," or some other good exclamation, sanctioned
by the parish vicar. As a general rule—proved
by many exceptions—the Kentish men seldom
swear very hard.

"Heart alive, young sir!" he exclaimed,
piling Hilary's plate, as he spoke, with the
jellied delights of cold pigeon pie; "you have
been the best man of the morning. Ah! don't
you be in a hurry, good wife. No tea, or
coffee our way, thank ye. No, nor any cask-
wash. We've worked a little too hard for that.
Mabel, whatever has come to you, that you
keep always out of the way so? And I never
saw you anigh the baskets. Now don't pipe
your eye, child. I'm not going to scold thee,
if thou didst have a little lie-a-bed. Here, take
this here key, child. A wink's as good as a
nod—ah, she knows pretty well what to do
with it."

For Mabel was glad to turn away as quickly as possible, after a little well-managed curtsy to Hilary, whom she had not seen for the morning —certainly through no fault of his—and without a word she went to the dresser (for in these busy times they took their breakfast wisely in the kitchen), and from the wooden crook un-hung a quaint little jug, with a narrow neck and a silver lip and handle. With this she set off down a quiet passage and some steps to a little stone cellar, where the choicest of the home-brewed ale was kept. Although it lay well beneath the level of the ground, and no ray of sun pierced the wired lattice, the careful mistress of the house had the barrels swathed closely with wetted sacks. The girl, with her neat frock gathered up—for she always was cleanliness itself—went carefully to the corner cask, and lifted the wet sack back from the head, lest any dirty water should have the chance of dripping upon her sleeve. Then she turned the tap, and a thin bright thread ran out of it sideways, being checked by some hops in the tube, perhaps, or want of air at the vent-peg. But Mabel held the jug with all patience, although her hand shook just a little.

" Now," said the Grower, to Hilary, when

she came back and placed the jug at her
father's side without a word, " Master Lorraine,
let me pour you a drop, not to be matched in
Kent; nor yet in all England, I do believe.
Home-grown barley, and home-grown hops,
and the soft water out of the brook that has
taken the air of the sky for seven mile or more,
without a drain anigh it. Ah, those brewers
can never do that! They must buy their malt,
and their musty hops, and pump up their water,
and boil it down, to get the flint stones out of.
it. But our brook hath cast the flint-stones and
the other pebbles all along. That makes a
sight of difference, sir. Every water is full of
stones, and if you pump it up from the spring,
the stones be all alive in it. But let it run seven
miles or eight, and then it is fit to brew with."

" Ah, to be sure. Now that explains a
great many things I never understood." Hilary
would have swallowed a camel, rather than
argue, at this moment.

" Young sir, just let me prove it to you.
Just see the colour it runs out, and the way the
head goes creaming! Lord, ha' mercy, if she
has gived us a glass, or a stag's horn from the
mantelpiece! Why, Mabel, child—Mabel, art
thou gone ? Nobody wants to poison thee."

"I think, sir, I saw your daughter go round the corner by the warming-pan, this side of where the broom hangs."

"Then all I can say is, she is daft. She worked very hard last week, poor thing. And yesterday she was a-moving always, when the Lord's day bids us rest. I must beg your pardon, Master Lorraine. Our Kentish maids always look after our guests. When I was at school, I read in the grammar that the moon always managed the women ; but now I do believe it is the comet. Let the comet come, say I. When the markets are so bad, I feel that I am ready to face almost anything. And now we must drink from the jug, I reckon !"

Hilary saw that his host was vexed ; but he felt quite certain in his own heart that Mabel could never be so rude, or show such resentment of any little over-sweetness on his part, as to go away in that sour earnest, and make the two of them angry. A dozen things might have happened to upset her, or turn her a little askew ; and her own father ought to know her better than he seemed to do. And lo, ere the Grower had quite finished grumbling, Mabel reached over his shoulder unseen, and set his own pet glass before him ; and then round

Hilary's side she slid, without ever coming too nigh to him, and the glass of honour of the house, cut in countless facets, twinkled, like the Pleiads, at him!

"Adorn me!" said the Grower; "now I call that a true good girl! Girls were always made, Master Lorraine, for the good of those around them. If anybody treats them any way else, they come to nothing afterwards. Mabel, dear, give me a kiss. You deserve it; and there it is for you. Now be off, like a good maid, and see what they be at in Vale Orchard, while Master Lorraine and I think a bit over these here two glasses."

The rest of the day was much too busy, and too much crowded with sharp eyes, for any fair chance of love-making. For they all set to at the cherry-trees, with ladders, crooks, and hanging baskets, and light boys to scale the more difficult antlers, strip them, and drop upon feather-beds. And though the sun broke hot and bright through the dew-cloud of the morning, and quickly drank the beaded freshness off the face of herb and tree, yet they picked, and piled, and packed (according to their sort and size) the long-stalked dancers that fringe the bough, and glance in the sun so ruddily.

"You must have had a deal too much of this," young Lovejoy said to Hilary, when the noon-day meal had been spread forth, and dealt with, in a patch of fern near a breezy clump: "if I had worked as you have done, my fingers would scarcely have been fit for a quill, this side of next Hilary term."

"My dear fellow, be not, I pray you, so violently facetious. The brain, when outraged, takes longer to resume its functions than the fingers do. Moreover, I trust that my fingers will hold something nobler than a quill, ere the period of my namesake."

"Sir Hilary charged at Agincourt; I hope you will do nothing of the sort;" said Gregory, with unwitting and unprecedented poetry.

"Lovejoy, my wits are unequal altogether to this encounter. The brilliancy of your native soil has burst out so upon you, that I must go back to the Southdown hills before I dare point a dart with you. Nevertheless, on your native soil, I beat you at picking cherries."

"That you do, and strawberries, too. And still more so at eating them! But if you please, you must stop a little. My mother begs, as a great favour, to have a little private talk with you."

Hilary's bright face lost its radiance, as his conscience pricked him. Was it about Mabel? Of course it must be. And what the dickens was he to say? He could not say a false thing. That was far below his nature. And he must own thàt he did love Mabel; and far worse than that—had done his utmost to drag that young and innocent Mabel into love with him. And if he were asked about his father—as of course he must be—on the word of a true man he must confess that his father would be sadly bitter if he married below his rank in life: also, that though he was the only son, there were very peculiar provisions in the settlement of the Lorraine estates, which might throw him entirely upon his own wits, if his father turned against him: also, that though his father was one of the very best men in the world, and the kindest and loftiest you could find; still there was about him something of a cold and determined substance. And worst of all (if the whole truth was to be shelled out, as he must unshell it), he knew in his heart that his father loved his sister's little finger more than all the members put together of his own too lively frame.

CHAPTER XVII.

VERY SHY THINGS.

MRS. LOVEJOY sat far away from all the worry, and flurry, and fun of picking, and packing, and covering up. She had never entirely given herself to the glories of fruit-growing ; and she never could be much convinced that any glory was in it. She belonged to a higher rank of life than any of such sons of Cain. Her father had been a navy-captain ; and her cousin was Attorney-General. This office has always been confounded, in the provincial mind, with rank in a less pugnacious profession. Even Mrs. Love-joy thought, when the land was so full of "militiamen," that her cousin was the General of the "Devil's Own" of the period. There-fore she believed herself to know more than usual about the law ; as well as the army, and of course the navy. And this high position in the legal army of so near a relation helped, no doubt, to foster hopes of the elevation of Gregory.

"I beg your pardon, Mr. Lorraine," she began, as Hilary entered the bower, to which she had just retired, "for calling you away from a scene, which you enjoy perhaps from its novelty; and where you make yourself, I am sure, so exceedingly active and useful. But I feared, as you must unluckily so very soon return to London, that I might have no other chance of asking what your candid opinion is upon a matter I have very near at heart."

"Deuce and all!" thought Hilary within himself, being even more vexed than relieved by this turn of incidence; "she is much cleverer than I thought. Instead of hauling me over the coals, she is going to give me the sack at once; and I didn't mean to go, for a week at least!" Mrs. Lovejoy enjoyed his surprise, as he stammered that any opinion he could form was entirely at her service.

"I am sure that you know what it is about. You must have guessed at once, of course, when I was rude enough to send for you, what subject is nearest to a mother's heart. I wish to ask you, what they think of my son Gregory, in London."

Lorraine, for the moment, was a little upset. His presence of mind had been worked so hard, that it was beginning to flutter and shift. And much as he liked his fellow-pupil, he had not begun to consider him yet as a subject of public excitement.

"I think—I really think," he said, while waiting for time to think more about it, "that he is going on as well as ever could be expected, ma'am."

If he had wanted to vex his hostess—which to his kind nature would have been one of the last things wanted—he scarcely could have hit on a phrase more fitted for his purpose.

"Why, Mr. Lorraine, that is exactly what the monthly nurses say! I hope you can say something a little better than that of Gregory."

"I assure you, Mrs. Lovejoy, nothing can be finer than the way he is going on. His attention, punctuality, steadiness, and everything else, leave nothing to be desired, as all the wine-merchants always say. Mr. Malahide holds him up as a pattern to be avoided, because he works so hard, and I think that he really ought to have country air, at this time of year, and in such weather, for a week, at the very shortest."

"Poor boy! Why should he overwork himself? Then you think that three days' change is scarcely enough to set him up again?"

"He wants at least a fortnight, ma'am. He has a sort of a hacking cough, which he does his best to keep under. And the doctors say that the smell of ink out of a pewter inkstand, and the inhaling of blotting-paper—such as we inhale all day—are almost certain, in hot weather, to root a tussis, or at any rate a pituita, inwards."

Mrs. Lovejoy was much impressed, and tenfold so when she tried to think what those maladies might be.

"Dear me!" she said : "it is dreadful to think of. I know too well what those sad complaints are. My dear grandfather died of them both. Do you think now, Mr Lorraine, that Mr. Malahide could be persuaded to spare you both for the rest of the week?"

"I scarcely think that he could, Mrs. Lovejoy. We are his right hand, and his left. Your son, of course, his dexter hand ; and my poor self the weaker member. Still, if you were to write to him, nicely (as of course you would be sure to write), he might make an effort to get on, with some of his inferior pupils."

"It shall be done, before the van goes—
by the very next mail, I mean. And if they
can spare you, do you think that you could put
up with your very poor quarters, for a few days
longer, Mr. Lorraine ? "

" I never was in such quarters before. And
I never felt so comfortable," he answered, with
a gush of truth, to expiate much small hypocrisy.
And thereby he settled himself for ever in her
very best graces. If Mrs. Lovejoy had any
pride—and she always told herself she had
none — that pride lay in her best feather-
beds.

A smile, quite worthy of her larger husband,
and of her pleasant homestead, spread itself
over her thoughtful face ; and Hilary, for the
first time, saw that her daughter, after all, was
born of her. What can be sweeter than a
smile, won from a sensible woman like that ?

" Then you give us some hope that we
may endeavour to keep you a few days more,
sir ? "

" The endeavour will be on my part," he
answered with his most elegant bow ; "as all
the temptation falls on me."

" I do hope that Mr. Malahide will do his
best to spare you both. Though to lose both

his right hand and his left hand must be very melancholy."

" To a lawyer, Mrs. Lovejoy, that is nothing. We think nothing of such trifles. We are ready to fight when we have no hands, nor even a leg to stand upon."

" Yes, to be sure, you live by fighting, as the poor sailors and soldiers do. The general of the attorneys now is my first cousin, once removed. Now can you tell me what opinion he has formed of my Gregory? Of course there must be a number of people trying to keep my poor boy back. Pressing him down, as they always do, with all that narrow jealousy. But his mother's cousin might be trusted to give him fair play, now, don't you think ?"

" One never can tell," answered Hilary ; " the faster a young fellow goes up the tree, the harder the monkeys pelt him. But if I only had a quarter of your son's ability, I would defy them all at once, from the Lord Chief-Justice downward."

" Oh no, now, Mr. Lorraine ; that really would be bad advice. He has not been called to the Bar as yet ; and he must remember that there are people many years in front of him. No, no ; let Gregory wait for his proper time

in its proper course, and steadily rise to the top
of the tree. With patience, Mr. Lorraine, you
know, with patience all things come to pass.
But I must go to the house at once, and write to
Mr. Malahide. Do you think that he would be
offended, if I asked him to accept a basket of
our choicest cherries and strawberries ? "

" I scarcely think that he would regard it as
a mortal injury ; especially if you were to put it
as a tribute from his grateful pupil, Hilary Lorraine."

" How kind of you to let me use your name!
And you have such influence with him, Gregory
is always telling me. No doubt he will accept
them so."

However, when she came to consider the
matter, Mrs. Lovejoy, with shameful treachery,
sent them as a little offering from that grateful pupil her own son: while she laid upon
Hilary all the burden of this lengthened
mitching-time ; as in the main perhaps was
just. Moreover, she took good care that
Shorne should have no chance of appearing in
chambers, as he was only too eager to do ;
for her shrewd sense told her that the sharp
wits there would find him a joy for ever, and
an enduring joke against Gregory.

.It is scarcely needful to say, perhaps, that throughout the rest of the week, Lorraine did his utmost to bring about snug little interviews with Mabel. And she, having made up her mind to keep him henceforth at his distance, felt herself bound by that resolution to afford him a glimpse or two, once in a way. For she really had a great deal to do; and it would have been cruel to deny her even the right to talk of it. And Hilary carried a basket so much better than anybody else, and his touch was so light, and he stepped here and there so obediently and so cleverly, and he always looked away so nicely, if anything happened to her frock—as now and then of course must be—that Mabel began every day to think how dreadfully she would miss him.

And then, as if it were not enough to please her ears, and eyes, and mind, he even contrived to conciliate the most grateful part of the human system, as well as the most intelligent. For on the Tuesday afternoon, the turn of the work, and the courses of fruit, led them near a bushy corner where the crafty brook stole though. As clever and snug a dingle as need be, for a pair of young people to drop accidentally out of sight and ear-shot.

For here, the corner of the orchard fell away, as a quarry does, yet was banked with grass, and ridges, so that children might take hands and run. But if they did so, they would be certain to come to grief at the bottom, unless they could clear at a jump three yards, which would puzzle most of them. For here the brook, without any noise, came under a bank· of good brown loam, with a gentle shallow slide, and a bottom content to be run over.

" Trout, as I'm a living sinner ! " cried Hilary with a fierce delight, as he fetched up suddenly on the brink, and a dozen streaks darted up the stream, like the throw of a threaded shuttle. " My prophetic soul, if I didn't guess it ! But I seem to forget almost everything. Why Miss Lovejoy, Miss Mabel Lovejoy, Mabel Miss Lovejoy (or any other form, insisting on the prefix despotically), have I known you for a century or more, and you never told me there were trout in the brook ! "

" Oh do let me see them ; please to show me where," cried Mabel, coming carefully down the steep, lest her slender feet should slip : " they are such dears, I do assure you. My mother and I are so fond of them. But my father says they are all bones and tail."

" I will show them to you with the greatest pleasure, only you must do just what I order you. They are very shy things, you know, almost as shy as somebody——"

" Mabel, Mabel, Mab, where are you ? " came a loud shout over the crest; and then Gregory's square shoulders appeared—a most unwelcome spectacle.

" Why, here I am to be sure," she answered; " where else do you suppose I should be ? The people must be looked after, I suppose. And if you won't do it, of course I must."

" I don't see any people to look after here, except indeed—however, you seem to have looked so hard, it has made you quite red in the face, I declare!"

" Now Greg, my boy," cried Hilary, suddenly coming to the rescue; " I called your sister down here on purpose to tell me what those things in the water are. They look almost like some sort of fish!"

" Why trout, Lorraine! Didn't you know that ? I thought that you were a great fisherman. If you like to have a try at them, I can fit you out. Though I don't suppose you could do much in this weather."

" Miss Lovejoy, did you ever taste a trout ? "

Hilary asked this question, as if not a word had yet passed on the subject.

"Oh yes," answered Mabel, no less oblivious; "my brother Charles used to catch a good many. They are such a treat to my dear mother, and so good for her constitution. But I don't think my father appreciates them."

"Allow me to help you up this steep rise. It was most inconsiderate of me to call you down, Miss Lovejoy."

"Pray do not mention it, Mr. Lorraine. Gregory, how rude you are to give Mr. Lorraine all this trouble! But you never were famous for good manners."

"If I meddle with them again," thought Gregory, "may I be 'adorned,' as my father says! However, I must keep a sharp look-out. The girl is getting quite independent; and I,—oh, I am to be nobody! I'll just go and see what Phyllis thinks of it."

But Mabel, who had not forgiven him yet for his insolent remarks about her cheeks, deprived him of even that comfort.

"Now Gregory dear, you have done nothing all day but wander about with cousin Phyllis. Just stay here for a couple of hours; if you can't work yourself, your looking on will make

the other people work. I am quite ashamed
of my inattention to Mr. Lorraine all the
afternoon. I am sure he must want a glass
of ale, after all he has gone through. And
while he takes it, I may be finding Charlie's
tackle for him. I know where it is, and you
do not. And Charlie left it especially under
my charge, you remember."

"That is the first I have heard of it.
However, if Lorraine wants beer, why so do
I. Send Phyllis out with a jug for me."

"Yes, to be sure, dear. To be sure. How
delighted she will be to come!"

"As delighted as you are to go," he
replied; but she was already out of hearing;
and all he took for his answer was an indignant
look from Hilary.

An excellent and most patient fisherman
used to say that the greatest pleasure of the
gentle art was found in the preparation to
fish. In the making of flies, and the knotting
of gut, and the softening of collars that have
caught fish, and the choosing of what to try
this time, and how to treat the river. The
treasures of memory glow again, and the
sparkling stores of hope awake to a lively
emulation.

Hilary's mind had securely landed every fish in the brook at least, and laid it at the feet of Mabel, ere ever his tackle was put to rights, and everything else made ready. At last he was at the very point of starting, with his ever high spirits at their highest pitch, when Mabel (who was scarcely a whit behind him in the excitement of this great matter) ran in for the fiftieth time at least, but this time wearing her evening frock. That frock was of a delicate buff, and she had a suspicion that it enhanced the clearness of her complexion, and the kind and deep loveliness of her eyes.

"You must be quite tired of seeing me, I am as sure as sure can be. But I am not come now to tie knots, or untie: and you quite understand all I know about trout, and all that my dear brother Charlie said. Ah, Mr. Lorraine, you should see him. Gregory is a genius, of course. But Charlie is not; and that makes him so nice. And his uniform, when he went to church with us—but to understand such things, you must see them. Still, you can understand this now, perhaps."

"I can understand nothing, when I look at you. My intellect seems to be quite absorbed in—in—I can't tell you in what."

" Then go, and absorb it in catching trout.
Though I don't believe you will ever catch
one.   It requires the greatest skill and patience,
when the water is bright, and the weather
dry.   So Charlie always said, when he could
not catch them.   Unless you take to a worm,
at least, or something a great deal nastier."

" A worm ! I would sooner lime them
almost.   Now you know me better than that,
I am sure."

" How should I know all the different
degrees of cruelty men have established ?
But I came to beg you just to take a little
bit of food with you.   Because you must be
away some hours, and you are sure to lose
your way."

" How wonderfully kind you are, Mabel !—
you must be Mabel now."

"Well, I suppose I have been Mabel ever
since they christened me.   But that has nothing
at all to do with it.   Only I came to make
you put this half of cold duck into your basket,
and this pinch of salt, and the barley-cake, and
a drop of our ale in this stone bottle.   To
drink it, you must do like this."

" Do you know what I shall be wanting,
every bit of the time, and for ever ? "

"Oh, the mustard—how stupid of me! But I hoped that the stuffing would do instead."

"Instead of the cold half duck, I shall want every atom of the whole duck, warm."

"Well, there they are, Mr. Lorraine, in the yard. Fourteen of them now coming up from the pond. Take one of them, if you can eat it raw. But my mother will make you pay for it."

"I will pay for my duck," he said, lifting his hat; "if it costs me every farthing I have, or shall ever have, in this world, or another."

And so he went fishing; and she ran upstairs, and softly cried, as she watched him going; and then lay down, with her hand on her heart.

CHAPTER XVIII.

THE KEY OF THE GATE.

THE trout knew nothing of all this. They
had not tasted a worm for a month, except
when a sod of the bank fell in, through cracks
of the sun, and the way cold water has of licking
upward. And even the flies had no flavour at
all; when they fell on the water, they fell flat,
and on the palate they tasted hot, even in under
the bushes.

Hilary followed a path through the meadows,
with the calm bright sunset casting his shadow
over the shorn grass, or up in the hedge-row, or
on the brown banks where the drought had
struck. On his back he carried a fishing-basket,
containing his bits of refreshment; and in his
right hand a short springy rod, the absent
sailor's favourite. After long council with
Mabel, he had made up his mind to walk up
stream, as far as the spot where two brooks

met, and formed body enough for a fly flipped
in very carefully to sail downward. Here he
began, and the creak of his reel, and the swish
of his rod, were music to him, after the whirl of
London life.

The brook was as bright as the best cut
glass, and the twinkles of its shifting facets only
made it seem more clear. It twisted about a
little, here and there; and the brink was fringed
now and then with something, a clump of loose-
strife, a tuft of avens, or a bed of flowering
water-cress, or any other of the many plants
that wash and look into the water. But the
trout, the main object in view, were most
objectionably too much in view. They scudded
up the brook, at the shadow of a hair, or even
the tremble of a blade of grass; and no pacific
assurance could make them even stop to be
reasoned with. "This won't do," said Hilary,
who very often talked to himself, in lack of a
better comrade: "I call this very hard upon
me. The beggars won't rise, till it is quite
dark. I must have the interdict off my tobacco,
if this sort of thing is to go on. How I should
enjoy a pipe just now! I may just as well sit
on a gate and think. No, hang it, I hate
thinking now. There are troubles hanging

over me, as sure as the tail of that comet grows. How I detest that comet! No wonder the fish won't rise. But if I have to strip, and tickle them in the dark, I won't go back without some for her."

He was lucky enough to escape the weight of such horrible poaching upon his conscience. For suddenly to his ears was borne the most melodious of all sounds, the flop of a heavy fish sweetly jumping after some excellent fly or grub.

" Ha, my friend!" cried Hilary; "so you are up for your supper, are you? I myself will awake right early. Still I behold the ring you made. If my right hand forget not his cunning, you shall form your next ring in the frying-pan."

He gave that fish a little time to think of the beauty of that mouthful, and get ready for another; the while he was putting a white moth on, in lieu of his blue-upright. He kept the grizzled palmer still for tail-fly, and he tried his knots, for he knew that this trout was a Triton.

Then, with a delicate sidling and stooping, known only to them that fish for trout in very bright water of the summer-time—compared with which art, the coarse work of the salmon-

fisher is as that of a scene-painter to Mr. Hol-
man Hunt's—with, or in, and by a careful
manner, not to be described to those who have
never studied it, Hilary won access of the
water, without any doubt in the mind of the
fish concerning the prudence of appetite. Then
he flipped his short collar in, not with a cast,
but a spring of the rod, and let his flies go
quietly down a sharpish run into that good
trout's hole. The worthy trout looked at them
both, and thought; for he had his own favourite
spot for watching the world go by, as the rest
of us have. So he let the grizzled palmer pass,
within an inch of his upper lip; for it struck
him that the tail turned up in a manner not
wholly natural, or at any rate unwholesome.
He looked at the white moth also, and thought
that he had never seen one at all like it. So he
went down under his root again, hugging him
self upon his wisdom, never moving a fin, but
oaring and helming his plump spotted sides
with his tail.

"Upon my word, it is too bad!" said Hilary,
after three beautiful throws, and exquisite
management down stream; "everything Kent
ish beats me hollow. Now, if that had been
one of our trout, I would have laid my life

upon catching him.   One more throw, however.
How would it be if I sunk my flies?   That
fellow is worth some patience."

While he was speaking, his flies alit on the
glassy ripple, like gnats in their love-dance;
and then by a turn of the wrist he played them
just below the surface, and let them go gliding
down the stickle, into the shelfy nook of shadow,
where the big trout hovered.   Under the
surface, floating thus, with the check of ductile
influence, the two flies spread their wings, and
quivered, like a centiplume moth in a spider's
web.   Still the old trout, calmly oaring, looked
at them both suspiciously.   Why should the
same flies come so often, and why should they
have such crooked tails, and could he be sure
that he did not spy the shadow of a human hat
about twelve yards up the water?   Revolving
these things he might have lived to a venerable
age—but for that noble ambition to teach,
which is fatal to even the wisest.   A young
fish, an insolent whipper-snapper, jumped in his
babyish way at the palmer, and missed it
through over-eagerness.   "I'll show you the
way to catch a fly," said the big trout to him;
" open your mouth like this, my son."

With that he bolted the palmer, and threw

up his tail, and turned to go home again. Alas!
his sweet home now shall know him no more.
For suddenly he was surprised by a most dis-
agreeable sense of grittiness, and then a keen
stab in the roof of his mouth. He jumped in
his wrath a foot out of the water, and then
heavily plunged to the depths of his hole.

"You've got it, my friend," cried Hilary, in
a tingle of fine emotions; "I hope the sailor's
knots are tied with professional skill and care.
You are a big one, and a clever one too. It is
much if I ever land you. No net, or gaff, or
anything. I only hope there are no stakes
here. Ah, there you go! Now comes the
tug."

Away went the big trout down the stream,
at a pace very hard to exaggerate, and after
him rushed Hilary, knowing that his line was
rather short, and that if it ran out, all was over.
Keeping his eyes on the water only, and the
headlong speed of the fugitive, headlong over a
stake he fell, and took a deep wound from
another stake. Scarcely feeling it, up he
jumped, lifting his rod, which had fallen flat,
and fearing to find no strain on it. "Aha! he
is not gone yet!" he cried, as the rod bowed
like a springle-bow.

He was now a good hundred yards down
the brook, from the corner where the fight
began. Through his swiftness of foot, and
good management, the fish had never been able
to tighten the line beyond yield of endurance.
The bank had been free from bushes, or haply
no skill could have saved him ; but now they
were come to a corner where a nutbush quite
over-hung the stream.

"I am done for now," said the fisherman ;
"the villain knows too well what he is about.
Here ends this adventure."

Full though he was of despair, he jumped
anyhow into the water, kept the point of his rod
close down, reeled up a little (as the fish felt
weaker), and just cleared the drop of the hazel-
boughs. The water flapped into the pockets of
his coat, and he saw red streaks flow downward.
And then he plunged out to an open reach of
shallow water and gravel slope.

"I ought to have you now," he cried ;
"though nobody knows what a rogue you are ;
and a pretty dance you have led me !"

Doubting the strength of his tackle to lift
even the dead weight of the fish, and much
more to meet his despairing rally, he happily
saw a little shallow gut, or backwater, where a

small spring ran out.   Into this, by a dexterous
turn, he rather led than pulled the fish, who was
ready to rest for a minute or two ; then he
stuck his rod into the bank, ran down stream,
and with his hat in both hands appeared at the
only exit from the gut.   It was all up now with
the monarch of the brook.   As he skipped and
jumped, with his rich yellow belly, and chaste
silver sides, in the green of the grass, joy and
glory of the highest merit, and gratitude, glowed
in the heart of Lorraine.   " Two and three
quarters you must weigh.   And at your very
best you are !   How small your head is !   And
how bright your spots are ! " he cried, as he
gave him the stroke of grace.   " You really
have been a brave and fine fellow.   I hope they
will know how to fry you."

While he cut his fly out of this grand trout's
mouth, he felt for the first time a pain in his
knee, where the point of the stake had entered
it.   Under the buckle of his breeches, blood
was soaking away inside his gaiters ; and then
he saw how he had dyed the water.   After
washing the wound, and binding it with dock-
leaves and a handkerchief, he followed the
stream through a few more meadows, for the
fish began to sport pretty well as the gloom of

the evening deepened ; so that by the time the gables of the old farm-house appeared (by the light of a young moon and the comet), Lorraine had a dozen more trout in his basket, silvery-sided and handsome fellows, though none of them over a pound, perhaps, except his first and redoubtable captive.

Herewith he resolved to be content; for his knee was now very sore and stiff, and the growing darkness baffled him; while having forgotten his food, as behoved him, he was conscious of an agreeable fitness for the supper-table. Here, of course, he had to tell, at least thrice over, his fight with the Triton; who turned the scale at three pounds and a quarter, and was recognized as an old friend and twice conqueror of the absent Charlie. Mrs. Lovejoy (as was to be expected) made a great ado about the gash in the knee—which really was no trifle —while Mabel said nothing, but blamed herself deeply for having equipped him to such mis-fortune.

For the next few days, Master Hilary was compelled to keep his active frame in rest, and quiet, and cosseting. Even the Grower, a man of strong manhood, accustomed to scythe-cuts, and chopper-hits, and pole-springs, admitted that this was a case for broth, and low feeding, and things that the women do. For if inflammation set up, the boy might have only one leg left for life. It was high time, however, for the son of the house to return to his beloved law-books; so that he tore himself away from Phyllis, and started in the van, about noon on Friday, having promised to send back by John Shorne all that his fellow-pupil wanted.

Lorraine soon found that his kind and quick hostess loved few things better than a cheerful, dutiful, and wholesome-blooded patient; and therefore he rejected with scorn all suggestions as to his need of a "proper doctor." And herein the Grower backed him up.

"Adorn me, if any one of them ever lays finger on me, any more than on my good father before me! They handle us when we are born, of course, and come to no manner of judgment; but if we let them handle us afterwards, we deserve to go out of the world before them."

This sound discretion (combined with the plentiful use of cold water and healing herbs) set Hilary on his legs again, in about eight or ten days' time. Meanwhile, he had seen very little of Mabel, whether through her fault or that of others he could not tell—only so it

was. Whenever his hostess was out of the way,
Phyllis Catherow, or else the housemaid, did
their best to supply her place; and very often
the Grower dropped in, to enjoy his pipe, and
to cheer his guest. By means of simple truth,
they showed him that he was no burden to
them, even at this busy time.

After all this, it was only natural that Hilary
should become much attached, as well as grateful, to his entertainers. Common formality was
dropped, and caste entirely sunk in hearty liking
and loving-kindness. And young Lorraine was
delighted to find how many pleasant virtues
flourished under the thatch of that old house,
uncoveted and undisturbed; inasmuch as their
absence was not felt in the mansions of great
people.

This affection for virtue doubtless made him
feel sadly depressed and lonely, when the time
at length arrived for quitting so much excellence.

"In the van he came, and in the van he
would go," he replied to all remonstrance; and
the Grower liked him all the better for his
loyalty to the fruit-coach. So it was settled
when Crusty John was "going up light" for a
Thursday morning, that Hilary should have a

mattress laid in the body of the vehicle, and a
horse-cloth to throw over him, if the night
should prove a cold one. For now a good drop
of rain had fallen, and the weather seemed on
the change awhile.

"I must catch you another dish of trout,"
said Hilary to Mrs. Lovejoy; "when shall I
have such a chance again? The brook is in
beautiful order now; and thanks to your wonderful skill and kindness, I can walk again quite
grandly."

"Yes, for a little way you can. But you
must be sure not to overdo it. You may fish
one meadow, and one only. Let me see. You
may fish the long meadow, Hilary; then you
will have neither stile nor hedge. The gate at
this end unlatches, mind. And I will send
Phyllis to let you out at the lower end, and to
see that you dare not go one step further. She
shall be there at half-past six. The van goes
at eight, you know, and we must sit down to
supper at seven exactly."

Upon this understanding he set forth, about
five o'clock in the afternoon, and meeting Miss
Catherow in the lane, he begged her, as an
especial favour, to keep out of Mrs. Lovejoy's
way for the next two hours only. Phyllis, a

good-natured girl on the whole (though a little too proud of her beauty perhaps), readily promised what he asked, and retired to a seat in the little ash coppice, to read a poem, and meditate upon the absent Gregory.

Lorraine was certainly in luck to-day, for he caught a nice basket of fish down the meadow; and towards the last stickle near the corner, where silver threads of water crossed, and the slanting sunshine cast a plaid of softest gold upon them, light footsteps came by the side of the hedge, and a pretty shadow fell near him.

"Miss Lovejoy!" cried Hilary: "how you amaze me! Why, I thought it was Phyllis who was coming to fetch me. I may call her Phyllis,—oh yes, she allows me. She is not so very ceremonious. But some people are all dignity."

"Now you want to vex me the very last thing. And they call you so sweet-tempered! I am so sorry for your disappointment about your dear friend Phyllis. But I am sure I looked for her everywhere, before I was obliged to come myself. Now I hope you have not found the poor little trout quite so hard to please as you are."

"At any rate, not so shy of me, as somebody

has been for a fortnight. Because I was in trouble, I suppose, and pain, and supposed to be groaning."

"How can you say such bitter things? It shows how very little you care—at least, that is not what I mean at all."

"Then, if you please, what is it that you do mean?"

"I mean that here is the key of the gate. And my father will expect you at seven o'clock."

"But surely you will have a look at my trout? They cannot bite, if I can."

He laid his fishing-creel down on the grass, and Mabel stooped over it to hide her eyes; which (in spite of all pride and prudence) were not exactly as she could have wished. But they happened to be exactly as Hilary wished, and catching a glimpse of them unawares, he lost all ideas except of them; and basely compelled them to look at him.

"Now, Mabel Lovejoy," he said, slowly, and with some dread of his own voice; "can you look me in the face, and tell me you do not care twopence for me?"

"I am not in the habit of being rude," she answered, with a sly glance from under her hat; "that I leave for other people."

"Well, do you like me, or do you not?"

"You do ask the most extraordinary questions. We are bound to like our visitors."

"I will ask a still more extraordinary question. Do you love me, Mabel?"

For a very long time he got no answer, except a little smothered sob, and two great tears that would have their way. "Darling Mabel, look up and tell me. Why should you be ashamed to say? I am very proud of loving you. Lovely Mabel, do you love me?"

"I—I—I am—very—much afraid—I almost do."

She shrank away from his arms and eyes, and longed to be left to herself for a little. And then she thought what a mean thing it was to be taking advantage of his bad leg. With that she came back, and to change his thoughts, said, "Show me a trout in the brook now, Hilary."

"You deserve to see fifty, for being so good. There, you must help me along, you know. Now just stand here and let me hold you, carefully and most steadily. No, not like that. That will never do. I must at least have one arm round you, or in you go, and I have to answer for your being 'drownded'!"

"Drowned! You take advantage now to make me so ridiculous. The water is scarcely six inches deep. But where are the little trout-sies?"

"There! There! Do you see that white stone? Now look at it most steadfastly, and then you are sure not to see them. Now turn your head like that, a little,—not too much, whatever you do. Now what do you see, most clearly?"

"Why, I see nothing but you and me, in the shadow of that oak tree, standing over the water, as if we had nothing better in the world to do!"

"We are standing together, though. Don't you think so?"

"Well, even the water seems to think so. And what can be more changeable?"

"Now look at me, and not at the water. Mabel, you know what I am."

"Hilary, I wish I did. That is the very thing that takes such a long time to find out."

"Now, did I treat you in such a spirit? Did I look at you, and think, 'here is a rogue I must find out'?"

"No, of course, you never did. That is not in your nature. At the same time, perhaps, it might not matter so long to you, as it must to me."

She met his glad eyes with a look so wistful, yet of such innocent trust (to assuage the harm of words), that Hilary might be well excused for keeping the Grower's supper waiting, as he did that evening.

CHAPTER XIX.

FOUR YOUNG LADIES.

THE excellent people of Coombe Lorraine as yet were in happy ignorance of all these fine doings on Hilary's part. Sir Roland knew only too well, of course, that his son and heir was of a highly romantic, chivalrous, and adventurous turn. At Eton and Oxford many little scrapes (which seemed terrible at the time) showed that he was sure to do his best to get into grand scrapes, as the landscape of his youthful world enlarged.

"Happen what will, I can always trust my boy to be a gentleman," his father used to say to himself, and to his only real counsellor, old Sir Remnant Chapman. Sir Remnant always shook his head; and then (for fear of having meant too much) said, "Ah, that is the one thing after all. People begin to talk a great deal too much about Christianity."

At any rate, the last thing they thought of was the most likely thing of all—that Hilary should fall in love with a good, and sweet, and simple girl, who, for his own sake, would love him, and grow to him with all the growth of love. "Morality"—whereby we mean now, truth, and right, and purity—was then despised in public, even more than now in private life. Sir Remnant thought it a question of shillings, how many maids his son led astray; and he pitied Sir Roland for having a son so much handsomer than his own.

Little as now he meddled with it, Sir Roland knew that the world was so; and the more he saw of it, the less he found such things go down well with him. The broad low stories, and practical jokes, and babyish finesse of oaths, invented for the ladies—many of which still survive in the hypocrisy of our good tongue—these had a great deal to do with Sir Roland's love of his own quiet dinner-table, and shelter of his pet child, Alice. And nothing, perhaps, except old custom and the traditions of friendship, could have induced him to bear, as he did, with Sir Remnant's far lower standard. Let a man be what he will, he must be moved one way or another by the folk he deals with. Even Sir

Roland (though so different from the people
around him) felt their thoughts around him
rambling, and very often touching him : and
he never could altogether help wanting to know
what they thought about him. So must the
greatest man ever "developed" have desired a
million-fold, because he lived in each one of the
million.

However, there were but two to whom Sir
Roland Lorraine ever yielded a peep of his
deeply treasured anxieties. One was Sir Remnant ; and the other (in virtue of his office, and
against the grain) was the Rev. Struan Hales,
his own highly respected brother-in-law.

Struan Hales was a man of mark all about
that neighbourhood. Everybody knew him ;
and almost everybody liked him. Because he
was a genial, open-hearted, and sometimes
noisy man ; full of life—in his own form of that
matter—and full of the love of life, whenever he
found other people lively. He hated every kind
of humbug, all revolutionary ideas, methodism,
asceticism, enthusiastic humanity, and exceedingly fine language. And though, like every one
else, he respected Sir Roland Lorraine for his
upright character, lofty honour, and clearness of
mind ; while he liked him for his generosity,

kindness of heart, and gentleness; on the other
hand he despised him a little, for his shyness
and quietude of life. For the rector of West
Lorraine loved nothing better than a good day
with the hounds, and a roaring dinner-party
afterwards. Nothing in the way of sport ever
came amiss to him; even though it did—as
no true sport does—depend for its joy upon
cruelty.

Here, in his red house on the glebe, under
the battlement of the hills, with trees and a
garden of comfort, and snug places to smoke a
pipe in, Mr. Hales was well content to live and
do his duty. He liked to hunt twice in a week,
and he liked to preach twice every Sunday.
Still he could not do either always; and no good
people blamed him.

Mrs. Hales was the sweetest creature ever
seen, almost anywhere. She had plenty to say
for herself, and a great deal more to say for
others; and if perfection were to be found, she
would have been perfection to every mind
except her own, and perhaps her husband's.
The rector used to say that his wife was an
angel, if ever one there were: and in his heart
he felt that truth. Still he did not speak to her
always, as if he were fully aware of being in

colloquy with an angel.   He had lived with her
" ever so long," and he knew that she was a
great deal better than himself ; but he had the
wisdom not to let her know it ; and she often
thought that he preached at her.   Such a thing
he never did.   No honest parson would ever do
it ; of all mean acts it would be the meanest.
Yet there are very few parsons' wives who are
not prepared for the chance of it ; and Mrs.
Hales knew that she " had her faults," and that
Mr. Hales was quite up to them.   At any rate,
here these good folk were, and here they meant
to live their lives out, having a pretty old place
to see to, and kind old neighbours to see to
them.   Also they had a much better thing—three
good children of their own; enough to make work
and pleasure for them, but not to be a perpetual
worry, inasmuch as they all were girls—three very
good girls, of their sort—thinking as they were
told to think, and sure to make excellent women.

Alice Lorraine liked all these girls.   They
were so kind, and sweet, and simple ; and
when they had nothing whatever to say, they
always said it so prettily.   And they never
pretended to interfere with any of her opinions,
or to come into competition with her, or to talk
to her father, when she was present, more than

she well could put up with. For she was a
very jealous child ; and they were well aware
of it; and they might let their father be her
mother's brother ten times over, before she
would hear of any "Halesy element"—as she
once had called it—coming into her family
more than it had already entered : and they
knew right well, while they thought it too bad,
that this young Alice had sadly quenched any
hopes any one of them might have cherished
of being a Lady Lorraine some day. She had
made her poor brother laugh over their tricks,
when they were sure that they had no tricks ;
and she always seemed to throw such a light
upon any little harmless thing they did. Still
they could afford to forget all that ; and they
did forget it; especially now, when Hilary
would soon be at home again.

It was now July; and no one had heard for
weeks from that same Hilary. But this made
no one anxious, because it was the well-known
manner of the youth. Sometimes they would
hear from him by every post, although the post
now came thrice in a week ; and then again for
weeks together, not a line would he vouchsafe.
And as a general rule, he was getting on better,
when he kept strict silence.

Therefore Alice had no load on her mind,
at all worth speaking of, while she worked in
her sloping flower-garden, early of a summer
afternoon. It was now getting on for St.
Swithin's day; and the sun was beginning to
curtail those brief attentions which he paid to
Coombe Lorraine. He still looked fairly at
it, as often as clouds allowed in the morning,
almost up to eight o'clock; and after that he
could still see down it, over the shoulder of
the hill. But he felt that his rays made no
impression (the land so fell away from him),
they seemed to do nothing but dance away
downward, like a lasher of glittering water.

Therefore, in this garden grew soft and
gentle-natured plants, and flowers of delicate
tint, that sink in the exhaustion of the sun-
glare. The sun, in almost every garden, sucks
the beauty out of all the flowers; he stains
the sweet violet even in March; he spots the
primrose and the periwinkle; he takes the
down off the heartsease blossom; he browns
the pure lily of the valley in May; and, after
that, he dims the tint of every rose that he
opens: and yet, in spite of all his mischief,
which of them does not rejoice in him?

The bold chase, cut in the body of the hill,

has rugged sides, and a steep descent for a quarter of a mile below the house—the cleft of the chalk on either side growing deeper towards the mouth of the coombe. The main road to the house goes up the coombe, passing under the eastern scarp, but winding away from it, here and there, to obtain a better footing. The old house, facing down the hill, stands so close to the head of the coombe, that there is not more than an acre or so of land behind and between it and the crest; and this is partly laid out as a courtyard, partly occupied by out-buildings, stables, and so on, and the ruinous keep ingloriously used as a lime-kiln; while the rest of the space is planted, in and out, with spruce and birch-trees, and anything that will grow there. Among them winds a narrow outlet to the upper and open Downs—too steep a way for carriage-wheels, but something in appearance betwixt a bridle-path and a timber-track, such as is known in those parts by the old English name, a "borstall."

As this led to no dwelling-house for miles and miles away, but only to the crown of the hills and the desolate tract of sheep-walks, ninety-nine visitors out of a hundred to the house came up the coombe, so that Alice from her flower-garden, commanding the course of the drive from the plains, could nearly always foresee the approach of any interruption. Here she had pretty seats under laburnums, and even a bower of jessamine, and a noble view all across the weald, even to the range of the North Downs; so that it was a pleasant place for all who love soft sward and silence, and . have time to enjoy that rare romance of the seasons—a hot English summer. ·

Only there was one sad drawback. Lady Valeria's windows straightly overlooked this pleasant spot, and Lady Valeria never could see why she should not overlook everything. Beyond and above all other things, she took it as her own special duty to watch her dear grand-daughter Alice; and now in her eighty-second year she was proud of her eyesight, and liked to prove its power.

" Here they come again !" cried Alice, talking to herself, or her rake, and trowel ; "will they never be content ? I told them on Monday that I knew nothing; and they will not believe it. I have a great mind to hide myself in my hole, like that poor rag-and-bone boy. It goes beyond my patience quite, to be cross-examined and not believed."

Those whom she saw coming up the steep road at struggling and panting intervals, were her three good cousins from the rectory— Caroline, Margaret, and Cecil Hales ; rather nice-looking and active girls, resembling their father in face and frame, and their excellent mother in their spiritual parts. The decorated period of young ladies—the time of wearing great crosses, and starving, and sticking as a thorn in the flesh of mankind, lay as yet in the happy future. A parson's daughters were as yet content to leave the parish to their father, helping him only in the Sunday-school; and for the rest of the week, minding their own dresses, or some delicate jobs of pastry, or gossip.

Though Alice had talked so of running away, she knew quite well that she never could do it, unless it were for a childish joke; and swiftly she was leaving now the pretty and petty world of childhood, sinking into that distance whence the failing years recover it. Therefore, instead of running away, she ran down the hill to meet her cousins; for truly she liked them decently.

" Oh, you dear, how are you ? How wonderfully good to come to meet us ! Madge,

I shall be jealous in a moment if you kiss my Alice so. Cecil—what are you thinking of ? Why, you never kissed your cousin Alice."

"Oh yes, you have all done it very nicely. What more could I wish ? " said Alice ; " but what could have made you come up the hill, so early in the day, dears ? "

"Well, you know what dear mamma is. She really fancied that we might seem (now there is so much going on) really unkind and heartless, unless we came up to see how you were. Papa would have come; but he feels it so steep, unless he is coming up to dinner ; and pony, you know — Oh, she did such a thing ! The wicked little dear, she got into the garden, and devoured £10 worth of the grand new flower, just introduced by the Duchess—' Dallia,' or ' Dellia,' I can't spell the name. And mamma was so upset that both of them have been unwell ever since."

"Oh, Dahlias ! " answered Alice, whose grapes were rather sour, because her father had refused to buy any; " flaunty things in my opinion. But Caroline, Madge, and Cecil, have you ever set eyes on my new rose ? "

Of course they all ran to behold the new rose ; which was no other than the " Persian

yellow," a beautiful stranger, not yet at home.
The countless petals of brilliant yellow folding
inward full of light, and the dimple in the
centre, shy of yielding inlet to its virgin gold,
and then the delicious fragrance, too refined
for random sniffers,—these and other delights
found entry into the careless beholders' mind.

"It makes one think of astrologers," cried
Caroline Hales; "I declare it does! Look
at all the little stars! It is quite like a celes-
tial globe."

"So it is, I do declare!" said Madge. But
Cecil shook her head. She was the youngest,
and much the prettiest, and by many degrees
the most elegant of the daughters of the
rectory. Cecil had her own opinion about
many things; but waited till it should be
valuable.

"It is much more like a cowslip-ball," Alice
answered, carelessly. "Come into my bower
now. And then we can all of us go to sleep."

The three girls were a little hot and thirsty,
after their climb of the chalky road; and a
bright spring ran through the bower, as they
knew, ready to harmonize with sherbet, sherry-
wine, or even shrub itself; as had once been
proved by Hilary.

"How delicious this is! How truly sweet!" cried the eldest, and perhaps most loquacious, Miss Hales; "and how nice of you always to keep a glass! A spring is such a rarity on these hills; papa says it comes from a different stratum. What a stratum is, I have no idea. It ought to be straight, one may safely say that; but it always seems to be crooked. Now, can you explain that, darling Alice? You are so highly taught, and so clever."

"Now, we don't want a lecture," said Madge, the blunt one; "the hill is too steep to have that at the top. Alice knows everything, no doubt, in the way of science, and all that. But what we are dying to know is what came of that grand old astrologer's business."

"This is the seventh or eighth time now," Alice answered, hard at bay, "that you will keep on about some little thing that the servants are making mountains of. My father best knows what it is. Let us go to his room and ask him."

"Oh no, dear! oh no, dear! How could we do that? What would dear uncle say to us? But come, now tell us. You do know something. Why are you so mysterious? Mystery is a thing altogether belonging to the dark

ages, now. We have heard such beautiful
stories, that we cannot manage to sleep at
night, without knowing what they are all about.
Now, do tell us everything. You may just
as well tell us every single thing. We are
sure to find it all out, you know; and then we
shall all be down on you. Among near relations, dear mamma says, there is nothing to
compare with candour."

"Don't you see, Alice," Madge broke in,
"we are sure to know sooner or later; and
how can it matter which it is?"

"To be sure," answered Alice, "it cannot
matter. And so you shall all know, later."

This made the three sisters look a little at
one another, quietly. And then, as a desperate
resource, Madge, the rough one, laid eyes upon
Alice, and, with a piercing look, exclaimed,
"You don't even understand what it means
yourself."

"Of course, I do not," answered Alice;
"how many times have I told you so; yet
you always want further particulars! Dear
cousins, now you must be satisfied with a conclusion of your own."

"I cannot at all see that," said Caroline.

"Really, you are too bad," cried Margaret.

"Do you think that this is quite fair?"
asked Cecil.

"You are too many for me, all of you,"
Alice answered, steadfastly. "Suppose I came
to your house and pried into some piece of
gossip about you, that I had picked up in the
village. Would you think that I had a right
to do it?"

"No, dear, of course not. But nobody
dares to gossip about us, you know. Papa
would very soon stop all that."

"Of course he would. And because my
father is too high-minded to meddle with it,
am I to be questioned perpetually? Come in
Caroline, come in, Margaret, come in, dear
Cecil; I know where papa is, and then you
can ask him all about it."

"I have three little girls at their first
sampler—such little sweets!" said Caroline;
"I only left them for half an hour, because
we felt sure you must want us, darling. It
now seems as if you could hold your own
in a cross-stitch we must not penetrate. It is
nothing to us. What could it be? Only
don't come, for goodness' sake, don't come
rushing down the hill, dear creature, to implore
our confidence suddenly."

"Dear creature!" cried Alice, for the moment borne beyond her young self-possession—"I am not quite accustomed to old women's words. Nobody shall call me a 'dear creature' except my father (who knows better) and poor old Nanny Stilgoe."

"Now, don't be vexed with them," Cecil stopped to say in a quiet manner, while the two other maidens tucked up their skirts, and down the hill went, rapidly; "they never meant to vex you, Alice; only you yourself must feel how dreadfully tantalizing it is to hear such sweet things as really made us afraid of our own shadows; and then to be told not to ask any questions!"

"I am sorry if I have been rude to your sisters," the placable Alice answered; "but it is so vexatious of them that they doubt my word so. Now, tell me what you have heard. It is wonderful how any foolish story spreads."

"We heard, on the very best authority, that the old astrologer appeared to you, descending from the comet in a fire-balloon, and warned you to prepare for the judgment-day, because the black-death would destroy in one night every soul in Coombe Lorraine; and as soon as you heard it you fainted away;

and Sir Roland ran up, and found you lying, as white as wax, in a shroud made out of the ancient gentleman's long foreign cloak."

"Then, beg Cousin Caroline's pardon for me. No wonder she wanted to hear more. And I must not be touchy about my veracity, after lying in my shroud so long. But truly I cannot tell you a word to surpass what you have heard already; nor even to come up to it. There was not one single wonderful thing —not enough to keep up the interest. I was bitterly disappointed; and so, of course, was every one."

"Cousin Alice," Cecil answered, looking at her pleasantly, "you are different from us, or, at any rate, from my sisters. You scarcely seem to know the way to tell the very smallest of small white lies. I am very sorry always; still I must tell some of them."

"No, Cecil, no. You need tell none; if you only make up your mind not to do it. You are but a very little older than I am, and surely you might begin afresh. Suppose you say at your prayers in the morning, 'Lord, let me tell no lie to-day!'"

"Now, Alice, you know that I never could do it. When I know that I mean to tell ever so many; how could I hope to be answered? No doubt I am a story-teller—just the same as the rest of us; and to pray against it, when I mean to do it, would be a very double-faced thing."

"To be sure it, would. It never struck me in that particular way before. But Uncle Struan must know best what ought to be done in your case."

"We must not make a fuss of trifles," Cecil answered, prudently; "papa can always speak for himself; and he means to come up the hill to do it, if Mr. Gates' pony is at home. And now I must run after them, or Madge will call me a little traitor. Oh, here papa comes, I do declare. Good-bye, darling, and don't be vexed."

"It does seem a little too bad," thought Alice, as the portly form of the rector, mounted on a borrowed pony, came round the corner at the bottom of the coombe, near poor Bonny's hermitage—"a little too bad that nothing can be done, without its being chattered about. And I know how annoyed papa will be, if Uncle Struan comes plaguing him again. We cannot even tell what it means ourselves; and whatever it means, it concerns us only. I do think curiosity is the worst, though it may be the smallest, vice. He expects to catch me, of course, and get it all out of me, as he declared he would. But sharp as his eyes are, I don't believe he can have managed to spy me yet. I will off to my rockwork, and hide myself, till I see the heels of his pony going sedately down the hill again."

With these words, she disappeared; and when the good rector had mounted the hill, "Alice, Alice!" resounded vainly from the drive among the shrubs and flowers, and echoed from the ramparts of the coombe.

CHAPTER XX.

A RECTOR OF THE OLDEN STYLE.

ONE part of Coombe Lorraine is famous for a seven-fold echo, connected by tradition with a tale of gloom and terror. Mr. Hales, being proud of his voice, put this echo through all its peals, or chime of waning resonance. It could not quite answer, " How do you do ? " with " Very well, Pat, and the same to you "— and its tone was rather melancholy than sprightly, as some echoes are. But of course a great deal depended on the weather, as well as on the time of day. Echo, for the most part, sleeps by daylight, and strikes her gong as the sun goes down.

Failing of any satisfaction here, the Rev. Struan Hales rode on. " Ride on, ride on ! " was his motto always ; and he seldom found it fail. Nevertheless, as he rang the bell (which he was at last compelled to do), he felt in the crannies of his heart some wavers as to the job he was come upon. A coarse nature often despises a fine one, and yet is most truly afraid of it. Mr. Hales believed that in knowledge of the world he was entitled to teach Sir Roland; and yet he could not help feeling how calmly any impertinence would be stopped.

The clergyman found his brother-in-law sitting alone, as he was too fond of doing, in his little favourite book-room, walled off from the larger and less comfortable library. Sir Roland was beginning to yield more and more to the gentle allurements of solitude. Some few months back he had lost the only friend with whom he had ever cared to interchange opinions, a learned parson of the neighbourhood, an antiquary, and an elegant scholar. And ever since that, he had been sinking deeper and deeper into the slough of isolation and privacy. For hours he now would sit alone, with books before him, yet seldom heeded, while he mused and meditated, or indulged in visions, mingled of the world he read of, and the world he had to deal with. As no less an authority than Dr. Johnson has it— " This invisible riot of the mind, this secret prodigality of being, is secure from detection, and fearless of reproach. The dreamer retires to his apartment, shuts out the cares and inter-

ruptions of mankind, and abandons himself to
his own fancy." And again—"This captivity
it is necessary for every man to break, who has
any desire to be wise or useful. To regain
liberty, he must find the means of flying from
himself; he must, in opposition to the Stoic
precept, teach his desires to fix upon external
things; he must adopt the joys and the pains
of others, and excite in his mind the want of
social pleasures and amicable communication."

Sir Roland Lorraine was not quite so bad
as the gentleman above depicted ; still he was
growing so like him, that he was truly sorry to
see the jovial face of his brother-in-law. For
his mind was set out upon a track of thought,
which it might have pursued until dinner-time.
But, of course, he was much too courteous to
show any token of interruption.

"Roland, I must have you out of this.
My dear fellow, what are you coming to ?
Books, books, books! As if you did not know
twice too much already! Even I find my flesh
falling away from me, the very next day after
I begin to punish it with reading."

"That very remark occurs in the book
which I have just put down. Struan, let me
read it to you."

"I thank you greatly, but would rather not. It is in Latin or Greek, of course. I could not do my duty as I do, if I lost my way in those dead languages. But I have the rarest treat for you; and I borrowed a pony, to come and fetch you. Such a badger you never saw! Sir Remnant is coming to see it, and so is old General Jakes, and a dozen more. We allow an hour for that, and then we have a late dinner at six o'clock. My daughters came up the hill, to fetch your young Alice to see the sport. But they had some blaze-up about some trifle; as the chittish creatures are always doing. And so pretty Alice perhaps will lose it. Leave them to their own ways, say I; leave them to their own ways, Sir Roland. They are sure to cheat us, either way; and they may just as well cheat us pleasantly."

"You take a sensible view of it, according to what your daughters are," Sir Roland answered, more sharply than he either meant or could maintain; and immediately he was ashamed of himself. But Mr. Hales was not thin of skin; and he knew that his daughters were true to him. "Well, well," he replied, "as I said before, they are full of tricks. At their age and sex it must be so. But a better and kinder team of maids is not to be found in thirteen parishes. Speak to the contrary who will."

"I know that they are very good girls," Sir Roland answered kindly; "Alice likes them very much; and so does everybody."

"That is enough to show what they are. Nobody ever likes anybody, without a great deal of cause for it. They must have their faults of course, we know; and they may not be quite butter-lipped, you know—still I should like to see a better lot, take them in and out, and altogether. Now you must come and see Fox draw that badger. I have ten good guineas upon it with Jakes; Sir Remnant was too shy to stake. And I want a thoroughly impartial judge. You never would refuse me, Roland, now?"

"Yes, Struan, yes; you know well that I will. You know that I hate and despise cruel sports: and it is no compliment to invite me, when you know that I will not come."

"I wish I had stayed at the bottom of the hill, where that young scamp of a boy lives. When will you draw that badger, Sir Roland, the pest of the Downs, and of all the county?"

"Struan, the boy is not half so bad as might

be expected of him.   I have thought once or twice that I ought to have him taught, and fed, and civilized."

" Send him to me, and I'll civilize him.   A born little poacher! I have scared all the other poachers with the comet; but the little thief never comes to church.   Four pair of birds, to my knowledge, nested in John Gates' vetches, and hatched well, too, for I spoke to John— where are they? Can you tell me where they are?"

" Well, Struan, I give you the shooting, of course; but I leave it to you to look after it. But it does seem too cruel to kill the birds, before they can fly, for you to shoot them."

" Cruel! I call it much worse than cruel. Such things would never be dreamed of upon a properly managed property."

" You are going a little too far," said Sir Roland, with one of his very peculiar looks; and his brother-in-law drew back at once, and changed the subject clumsily.

" The shooting will do well enough, Sir Roland; I think, however, that you may be glad of my opinion upon other matters.   And that had something to do with my coming."

" Oh, I thought that you came about the

badger, Struan. But what are these, even more
serious matters ? "

"Concerning your dealings with the devil,
Roland. Of course, I never listen to anything
foolish. Still, for the sake of my parish, I am
bound to know what your explanation is. I
have not much faith in witchcraft; though in
that perhaps I am heterodox; but we are bound
to have faith in the devil, I hope."

"Your hope does you credit," Sir Roland
answered; "but for the moment I fail to see
how I am concerned with this orthodoxy."

"Now, my dear fellow, my dear fellow, you
know as well as I do, what I mean. Of course
there is a great deal of exaggeration ; and
knowing you so well, I have taken on myself to
deny a great part of what people say. ' But you
know the old proverb, 'No smoke without
fire ;' and I could defend you so much better, if
I knew what really had occurred. And besides
all that, you must feel, I am sure, that you are
not treating me with that candour which our
long friendship and close connection entitle me
to expect from you."

"Your last argument is the only one re-
quiring any answer. Those based on religious, social, and even parochial grounds, do not

apply to this case at all.   But I should be sorry
to vex you, Struan, or keep from you anything
you claim to know in right of your dear sister.
This matter, however, is so entirely confined to
those of our name only; at the same time so
likely to charm all the gossips who have made
such wild guesses about it; and after all it is
such a trifle, except to a superstitious mind;
that I may trust your good sense to be well
content to hear no more about it, until it comes
into action—if it ever should do so."

"Very well, Sir Roland, of course you
know best.   I am the last man in the world
to intrude into family mysteries.   And my very
worst enemy (if I have one) would never dream
of charging me with the vice of curiosity."

"Of course not.   And therefore you will be
well pleased that we should drop this subject.
Will you take white wine, or red wine, Struan?
Your kind and good wife was quite ready to
scold me, for having forgotten my duty in that,
the last time you came up the hill."

"Ah, then I walked: to-day I am riding.
I thank you, I thank you, Sir Roland; but the
General and Sir Remnant are waiting for me."

"And, most important of all, the badger.
Good-bye, Struan; I shall see you soon."

"I hardly know whether you will or not," the rector answered testily; "this is the time when those cursed poachers scarcely allow me a good night's rest. And to come up this hill; and hear nothing at the top! It is too bad at my time of life! After two services every Sunday, to have to be gamekeeper all the week!"

"At your time of life!" said Sir Roland, kindly: "why, you are the youngest man in the parish, so far as life and spirits go. To-day you are not yourself at all. Struan, you have not sworn one good round oath!"

"Well, what can you expect, Roland, with these confounded secrets held over one? I feel myself many pegs down to-day. And that pony trips so abominably. Perhaps, after all, I might take one glass of red wine, before I go down the hill."

"It is a duty you owe to the parish. Now come, and let me try to find Alice, to wait upon you. Alice is always so glad to see you."

"And I am always so glad to see her. How narrow your doors are in these old houses! Those Normans must have been a skewer-shouldered lot. Now, Roland, if I have said anything harsh, you will make all allowance for me, of course ; because you know the reason."

"You mean that you are a little disappointed——"

"Not a bit of it. Quite the contrary. But after such weather as we've had, and nothing but duty, duty, to do—one is apt to get a little crotchety. What kind of sport can be got anywhere ? The landrail-shooting is over, of course, and the rabbits are running in families ; the fish are all sulky, and the water low, and the sea-trout not come up yet. There are no young hounds fit to handle yet ; and the ground cracks the heels of a decent hack. One's mouth only waters at oiling a gun ; all the best of the cocks are beginning to mute ; and if one gets up a badger-bait, to lead to a dinner-party, people will come, and look on, and make bets, and then tell the women how cruel it was ! And with all the week thus, I am always expected to say something new, every Sunday morning ! "

"Nay, nay, Struan. Come now ; we have never expected that of you. But here comes Alice, from her gardening work ! Now, she does look well ; don't you think she does ? "

"Not a rose in June, but a rose in May ! "

the rector answered gallantly, kissing his hand to his niece, and then with his healthy bright lips saluting her: " you grow more and more like your mother, darling. Ah, when I think of the bygone days, before I had any wife, or daughters, things occur to me that never——"

" Go and bait your badger, Struan, after one more glass of wine."

CHAPTER XXI.

NATURE appears to have sternly willed that no
man shall keep a secret. There is a monster,
here and there to be discovered, capable of not
even whispering anything ; but he ought to
expect to be put aside, in our estimate of
humanity. And lest he should be so, the
powers above provide him, for the most part,
with a wife of fecund loquacity.

A word is enough on such parlous themes ;
and the least said, the soonest mended. What
one of us is not exceeding wise, in his own, or
his wife's opinion ? What one of us does not
pretend to be as " reticent " as Minerva's owl ;
and yet in his heart confess that a secret is apt
to fly out of his bosom ?

Nature is full of rules ; and if the above
should happen to be one of them, it was illus-
trated in the third attack upon Sir Roland's

secrecy. For scarcely had he succeeded in baffling, without offending, his brother-in-law, when a servant brought him a summons from his mother, Lady Valeria.

According to all modern writers, whether of poetry or prose, in our admirable language, the daughter of an earl is always lovely, graceful, irresistible; almost to as great an extent as she is unattainable. This is but a natural homage on the part of nature to a power so far above her; so that this daughter of an Earl of Thanet had been, in every outward point, whatever is delightful. Neither had she shown any slackness in turning to the best account these notable gifts in her favour. In short, she had been a very beautiful woman, and had employed her beauty well, in having her own will and way. She had not married well, it is true, in the opinion of her compeers; but she had pleased herself, and none could say that she had lowered her family. The ancestors of Lord Thanet had held in villeinage of the Lorraines, some three or four hundred years after the Conquest, until, from being under so gentle a race, they managed to get over them.

Lady Valeria knew all this; and feeling as all women feel, the ownership of her husband

(active, or passive, whichever it be), she threw
herself into the nest of Lorraine, and having no
portion, waived all other obligation to parental
ties. This was a noble act on her part, as her
husband always said. He, Sir Roger Lorraine,
lay under her thumb, as calmly as need be ; yet
was pleased as the birth of children gave some
distribution of pressure. For the lady ruled
the house, and lands, and all that was therein,
as if she had brought them under her settlement.

Although Sir Roger had now been sleeping,
for a good many years, with his fathers, his
widow, Lady Valeria, showed no sign of any
preparation for sleeping with her mothers. Now
in her eighty-second year, this lady was as
brisk and active, at least in mind if not in body,
as half a century ago she had been. Many
good stories (and some even true) were told
concerning her doings and sayings in the time
of her youth and beauty. Doings were always
put first, because for these she was more famous,
having the wit of ready action more than of
rapid words, perhaps. And yet in the latter she
was not slack, when once she had taken up the
quiver of the winged poison. She had seen so
much of the world, and of the loftiest people
that dwell therein—so far at least as they were

to be found at the Court of George the Second
—that she sat in an upper stratum now over all
she had to deal with. And yet she was not of
a narrow mind, when unfolded out of her
creases. Her set of rooms was the best in
the house, of all above the ground-floor at least;
and now she was waiting to receive her son,
with her usual little bit of state. For the last
five years she had ceased to appear at the
table where once she ruled supreme; and the
servants, who never had blessed her before,
blessed her and themselves for that happy
change. For she would have her due, as
firmly and fairly (if not a trifle more so), as
and than she gave the same to others, if unde-
manded.

In her upright seat she was now beginning
—not to chafe, for such a thing would have
been below her—but rather to feel her sense of
right and duty (as owing to herself) becoming
more and more grievous to her the longer she
was kept waiting. She had learned long ago
that she could not govern her son as absolutely
as she was wont to rule his father; and having
a clearer perception of her own will than of any
large principles, whenever she found him im-
movable, she set the cause down as prejudice.

Yet by feeling her way among these prejudices
carefully, and working filial duty hard, and
flying as a last resort to the stronghold of her
many years, she pretty nearly always managed
to get her own way in everything.

But few of those who pride themselves on
their knowledge of the human face would have
perceived in this lady's features any shape of
steadfast will. Perhaps the expression had
passed away, while the substance settled inwards ; but however that may have been, her
face was pleasant, calm, and gentle. Her
manner also to all around her was courteous,
kind, and unpretending ; and people believed
her to have no fault, until they began to deal
with her. Her eyes, not overhung with lid, but
delicately set and shaped, were still bright, and
of a pale blue tint ; her forehead was not remarkably large, but straight and of beautiful
outline ; while the filaments of fine wrinkles
took, in some lights, a cast of silver from snowy
silkiness of hair. For still she had abundant
hair, that crown of glory to old age ; and like a
young girl, she still took pleasure in having it
drawn through the hands, and done wisely, and
tired to the utmost vantage.

Sir Roland came into his mother's room

with his usual care and diligence. She with ancient courtesy rose from her straight-backed chair, and offered him one little hand, and smiled at him; and from the manner of that smile he knew that she was not by any means pleased, but thought it as well to conciliate him.

"Roland, you know that I never pay heed," she began, with a voice that shook just a little, "to rumours that reach me through servants, or even allow them to think of telling me."

"Dear mother, of course you never do. Such a thing would be far beneath you."

"Well, well, you might wait till I have spoken, Roland, before you begin to judge me. If I listen to nothing, I must be quite unlike all the other women in the world."

"And so you are. How well you express it! At last you begin to perceive, my dear mother, what I perpetually urge in vain—your own superiority."

What man's mother can be expected to endure mild irony, even half so well as his wife would?

"Roland, this manner of speech,—I know not what to call it, but I have heard of it among foreign people years ago,—whatever it is, I beg you not to catch it from that boy Hilary."

"Poetical justice!" Sir Roland exclaimed; for his temper was always in good control, by virtue of varied humour; "this is the self-same whip wherewith I scourged little Alice, quite lately! Only I feel that I was far more just."

"Roland, you are always just. You may not be always wise, of course; but justice you have inherited from your dear father, and from me. And this is the reason why I wish to know what is the meaning of the strange reports, which almost any one, except myself, would have been sure to go into, or must have been told of long ago. Your thorough truthfulness I know. And you have no chance to mislead me now."

"I will imitate, though perhaps I cannot equal, your candour, my dear mother, by assuring you that I greatly prefer to keep my own counsel in this matter."

"Roland, is that your answer? You admit that there is something important, and you refuse to let your own mother know it!"

"Excuse me, but I do not remember saying anything about 'importance.' I am not superstitious enough to suppose that the thing can have any importance."

"Then why should you make such a fuss

about it? Really, Roland, you are sometimes very hard to understand."

"I was not aware that I had made a fuss," Sir Roland answered, gravely; "but if I have, I will make no more. Now, my dear mother, what did you think of that extraordinary bill of Bottler's?"

"Bottler, the pigman, is a rogue," said her ladyship, peremptorily; "his father was a rogue before him; and those things run in families. But surely you cannot suppose that this is the proper way to treat the subject."

"To my mind a most improper way—to condemn a man's bill on the ground that his father transmitted the right to overcharge!"

"Now, my dear son," said Lady Valeria, who never called him her son at all, unless she was put out with him, and her "dear son" only when she was at the extremity of endurance— "my dear son, these are sad attempts to disguise the real truth from me. The truth I am entitled to know, and the truth I am resolved to know. And I think that you might have paid me the compliment of coming for my advice before."

Finding her in this state of mind, and being unable to deny the justice of her claim, Sir

Roland was fain at last to make a virtue of necessity, while he marvelled (as so many have done) at the craft of people in spying things, and espying them always wrongly.

" Is that all ? " said Lady Valeria, after listening carefully ; " I thought there must have been something a little better than that, to justify you in making it such a mystery. Nothing but a dusty old document, and a strange-looking package, or case like a cone ! However, I do not blame you, my dear Roland, for making so small a discovery. The old astrologer appears to me to have grown a little childish. Now, as I keep to the old-fashioned hours, I will ask you to ring the bell for my tea ; and while it is being prepared, you can fetch me the case itself, and the document to examine."

" To be sure, my dear mother, if you will only promise to obey the commands of the document."

" Roland, I have lived too long ever to promise anything. You shall read me these orders, and then I can judge."

" I will make no fuss about such a trifle," he answered, with a pleasant smile ; " of course you will do what is honourable."

Surely men, although they deny so fero-
ciously this impeachment, are open at times to
at least a little side-eddy of curiosity ; Sir
Roland, no doubt, was desirous to know what
were the contents of that old case, which Alice
had taken for a " dirty cushion," as it lay at the
back of the cupboard in the wall ; while his
honour would not allow him comfortably to dis-
obey the testator's wish. At the same time he
felt, every now and then, that to treat such a
matter in a serious light, was a proof of superstition, or even childishness, on his part. And
now, if his mother should so regard it, he was
not at all sure that he ought to take the unpleasant course of opposing her.

CHAPTER XXII.

A MALIGNANT CASE.

SIR ROLAND smiled at his mother's position, and air of stern attention, as he came back from his book-room with a small but heavy oaken box. This he placed on a chair, and, without any mystery, unlocked it. But no sooner had he flung back the lid and shown the case above described, than he was quite astonished at the expression of Lady Valeria's face. Something more than fear, a sudden terror, as if at the sight of something fatal, had taken the pale tint out of her cheeks, and made her fine forehead quiver.

"Dear mother, how foolish I am," he said, "to worry you with these trifles! I wish I had kept to my own opinion——"

"It is no trifle; you would have been wrong to treat it as a trifle. I have lived a

long life, and seen many strange things; it
takes more than a trifle to frighten me."

For a minute or two she lay back, and was
not fit to speak or be spoken to; only she
managed to stop her son from ringing for her
maid or the housekeeper. He had never
beheld her alarmed before, and could scarcely
make out her signs to him that she needed no
attendance.

Like most men who are at all good and
just, Sir Roland was prone to think softly and
calmly, instead of acting rapidly; and now his
mother, so advanced in years, showed less
hesitation than he did. Recovering, ere long,
from that sudden shock, she managed to smile
at herself and at his anxiety about her.

"Now Roland, I will not meddle with this
formidable and clumsy thing. It seems to be
closed most jealously. It has kept for two
centuries, and may keep for two more, so far
as I am concerned. But if it will not be too
troublesome to you, I should like to hear what
is said about it."

"In this old document, madam? Do you
see how strangely it has been folded? Whoever did that knew a great deal more than now
we know about folding."

"The writing to me seems more strange than the folding. What a cramped hand! In what language is it written?"

"In Greek, the old Greek character, and the Doric dialect. He seems to have been proud of his classic descent, and perhaps Dorian lineage. But he placed a great deal too much faith in the attainments of his descendants. Poor Sedley would have read it straight off, I daresay; but the contractions, and even some of the characters, puzzled me dreadfully. I have kept up, as you know, dear mother, whatever little Greek I was taught, and perhaps have added to it; but my old Hedericus was needed a great many times, I assure you, before I got through this queer document; and even now I am not quite certain of the meaning of one or two passages. You see at the head a number of what I took at first to be hieroglyphics of some kind or other; but I find that they are astral or sidereal signs, for which I am none the wiser, though perhaps an astronomer would be. This, for instance, appears to mean the conjunction of some two planets, and this——"

"Never mind them, Roland. Read me what you have made out of the writing."

"Very well, mother. But if I am at fault, you must have patience with me, for I am not perfect in my lesson yet. Thus it begins :—

"'Behold, ye men, who shall be hereafter, and pay heed to this matter. A certain Carian, noble by birth and of noble character, to whom is the not inglorious name, Agasicles Syennesis, hath lived not in the pursuit of wealth, or power, or reputation, but in the unbroken study of the most excellent arts and philosophies. Especially in the heavenly stars, and signs of the everlasting kosmos, hath he disciplined his mind, and surpassed all that went before him. There is nothing like self-praise, is there, now, dear mother?"

"I have no doubt that he speaks the truth," answered the Lady Valeria : "I did not marry into a family accustomed to exaggerate."

"Then what do you think of this? 'Not only in intellect and forethought, but also in goodwill and philanthropy, modesty, and self-forgetfulness, did this man win the prize of excellence; and he it is who now speaks to you Having lived much time in a barbarous island, cold, and blown over with vaporous air, he is no longer of such a sort as he was in the land of the fair afternoons. And there is when

it is to his mind a manifest and established
thing, that the gates of Hades are open for him,
and the time of being no longer. But he holds
this to be of the smallest difference, if only the
gods produce his time to the perfect end of all
the things lying now before him.'"

"How good, and how truly pious of him,
Roland! Such a man's daughter never could
have had any right to run away from him."

"My dear mother, I disagree with you, if
he always praised himself in that style. But
let him speak for himself again, as he seems to
know very well how to do : 'These things have
not been said, indeed, for the sake of any
boasting, but rather to bring out thoroughly
forward the truth in these things lying under,
as if it were a pavement of adamant. Now,
therefore, know ye, that Agasicles, carefully
pondering everything, has found (so to say the
word) an end to accomplish, and to abide in.
And this is no other thing, than to save the
generations descended from him, from great evil
fortunes about to fall, by the ill-will of some
divinity, at a destined time, upon them. For a
man, of birth so renowned and lofty, has not
been made to resemble a hand-worker, or a
runaway slave; but has many stars regarding

him, from many generations. And now he per-
ceives, that his skill and wisdom were not given
to him to be a mere personal adornment; but
that he might protect his descendants, to the
remote futurity.   To him, then—it having been
revealed, that in the seventh generation hence,
as has often come to pass with our house, or
haply in the tenth (for the time is misty), a great
calamity is bound to happen to those born afar
off from Syennesis—the sage has laboured
many labours, though he cannot avert, at least
to make it milder, and to lessen it.   He has
not, indeed, been made to know, at least up to
the present time, what this bane will be; or
whether after the second, or after the third
century from this period.   But knowing the
swiftness of evil chance, he expects it at the
earlier time; and whatever its manner or kind
may be, Agasicles in all his discoveries has
discovered no cure for human evils, save that
which he now has shut up in a box.   This box
has been so constructed, that nothing but dust
will meet the greedy eyes of any who force it
open, in the manner of the tomb of Nitocris.
But if it be opened with the proper key, and
after the proper interval, when the due need
has arisen—there will be a fairer sight than
ever broke upon mortal eyes before.'

" There mother, now, what do you think of all that ? I am quite out of breath with my long translation, and I am not quite sure of all of it. For instance, where he says——"

" Roland," his mother answered quickly, " I am now much older than the prince, according to tradition, can have been. But I make no pretence to his wisdom; and I have reasons of my own for wondering. What have you done with the key of that case ? "

" I have never seen it. It was not in the closet. And I meant to have searched, throughout his room, until I found out the meaning of this very crabbed postscript—'That fool, Memel, hath lost the key. It will cost me months to make another. My hands now tremble, and my eyes are weak. If there be no key found herewith, let it be read that Nature, whom I have vanquished, hath avenged herself. Whether, or no, have I laboured in vain ? Be blest now, and bless me, my dear descendants.'"

" That appears to me," said the Lady Valeria, being left in good manners by her son, to express the first opinion, " to be of the whole of this strange affair the part that is least satisfactory.'"

" My dear mother, you have hit the mark.

What satisfaction can one find in having a case without a key, and knowing that if we force it open there will be nothing but dust inside? Not a quarter so good as a snuff-box. I must have a pinch, my dear mother, excuse me, while you meditate on this subject. You are far more indulgent in that respect than little Alice ever is."

"All gentlemen take snuff," said the lady; "who is Alice to lay down the law? Your father took a boxful three times a week. Roland, you let that young girl take great liberties with you."

"It is not so much that I let her take them. I have no voice in the matter now. She takes them without asking me. Possibly that is the great calamity foretold by the astrologer. If not, what other can it be, do you think?"

"Not so," she answered, with a serious air, for all her experience of the witty world had left her old age quite dry of humour; "the trouble, if any is coming, will not be through Alice, but through Hilary. Alice is certainly a flighty girl, romantic, and full of nonsense, and not at all such as she might have been, if left more in my society. However, she never has thought it worth while to associate much with her grandmother; the result of which is that her manners are unformed, and her mind is full of nonsense. But she has plenty, and (if it were possible) too much, of that great preservative—pride of birth. Alice may come to affliction herself; but she never will involve her family."

"Any affliction of hers," said Sir Roland, "will involve at least her father."

"Yes, yes, of course. But what I mean is the honour and rank of the family. It is my favourite Hilary, my dear, brave, handsome Hilary, who is likely to bring care on our heads, or rather upon your head, Roland; my time, of course, will be over then, unless he is very quick about it."

"He will not be so quick as that, I hope," Sir Roland answered, with some little confusion of proper sentiments; "although in that hotbed of mischief, London, nobody knows when he may begin. However, he is not in London at present, according to your friend Lady de Lampnor. I think you said you had heard so from her."

"To be sure, Mr. Malahide told her himself. The dear boy has overworked himself so, that he has gone to some healthy and quiet place, to recruit his exhausted energies."

" Dear me," said Sir Roland, " I could never believe it, unless I knew from experience, what a very little work is enough to upset him. To write a letter to his father, for instance, is so severe an exertion, that he requires a holiday the next day."

" Now, Roland, don't be so hard upon him. You would apprentice him to that vile law, which is quite unfit for a gentleman. I am not surprised at his being overcome by such odious labour; you would not take my advice, remember, and put him into the only profession fit for one of his birth—the army. Whatever happens, the fault is your own. It is clear, however, that he cannot get into much mischief where he is just now—a rural and quiet part of Kent, she says. It shows the innocence of his heart to go there."

" Very likely. But if he wanted change, he might have asked leave to come home, I think. However, we shall have him here soon enough."

" How you speak, Roland ! Quite as if you cared not a farthing for your only son ! It must be dreadfully galling to him, to see how you prefer that Alice."

" If he is galled, he never winces," answered Sir Roland, with a quiet smile ; " he is the most careless fellow in the world."

"And the most good-natured, and the most affectionate," said Lady Valeria, warmly; "nothing else could keep him from being jealous, as nine out of ten would be. However, I am tired of talking now, and on that subject I might talk for ever. Take away that case, if you please, and the writing. On no account would I have them left here. Of course you will lock them away securely, and not think of meddling with them. What is that case made of?"

"I can scarcely make out. Something strong and heavy. A mixture, I think, of shagreen and some metal. But the oddest thing of all is the keyhole. It is at the top of the cone, you see, and of the strangest shape, an irregular heptagon, with some rare complication of points inside. It would be next to impossible to open this case, without shattering it altogether."

"I do not wish to examine the case, I wish to have it taken away, my son. There, there, I am very glad not to see it; although I am sure I am not superstitious. We shall do very well, I trust, without it. I think it is a most extraordinary thing that your father never consulted me, about the writing handed down to you.

He must have been bound by some pledge not to do so. There, Roland, I am tired of the subject."

With these words, the ancient lady waved her delicate hand, and dismissed her son, who kissed her white forehead, according to usage, and then departed with case and parchment locked in the oaken box again. But the more he thought over her behaviour, the more he was puzzled about it. He had fully expected a command to open the case, at whatever hazard; and perhaps he had been disappointed at receiving no such order. But above all, he wanted to know why his mother should have been taken aback, as she was, by the sight of these little things. For few people, even in the prime of life, possessed more self-command and courage than Lady Valeria, now advancing into her eighty-second year.

CHAPTER XXIII.

THE BAITER BAITED.

At the top of the hill, these lofty themes were being handled worthily; while, at the bottom, little cares had equal glance of the democrat sun, but no stars allotted to regard them. In plain English,—Bonny and Jack were as busy as their betters. They had taken their usual round that morning, seeking the staff of life— if that staff be applicable to a donkey—in village, hamlet, and farmhouse, or among the lanes and hedges. The sympathy and good-will between them daily grew more intimate, and their tastes more similar; so that it scarcely seemed impossible that Bonny in the end might learn to eat clover, and Jack to rejoice in money. Open air, and roving life, the ups and downs of want and weal, the freedom of having nothing to lose, and the joyful luck of finding things—these, and perhaps a little spice of un-

known sweetness in living at large on their
fellow-creatures' labours, combined to make
them as happy a pair, as the day was long, or
the weather good. In the winter—ah! why
should we think of such trouble? Perhaps
there will never be winter again.

At any rate, Bonny was sitting in front of
the door of his castle (or rather in front of the
doorway, because he was happy enough not to
have a door), as proud and contented as if there
could never be any more winter of discontent.
He had picked up a hat in a ditch that day, lost
by some man going home from his Inn; and
knowing from his patron, the pigman Bottler,
that the surest token of a blameless life is to be
found in the hat of a man, the boy, stirred by
the first heave of ambition, had put on this hat,
and was practising hat-craft (having gone with
his head as it was born hitherto), to the utter
surprise, and with the puzzled protest, of his
beloved donkey. It was a most steady church-
going hat of the chimney-pot order (then newly
imported into benighted regions, but now of
the essence of a godly life all over this free
country), neither was it such a shocking bad hat
as a man would cast away, if his wife were
near. For Bonny's young head it was a world

too wide, but he had padded it with a black-
bird's nest; and though it seemed scarcely in
harmony with his rakish waistcoat, and bare red
shanks (spread on the grass for exhibition, and
starred with myriad furze and bramble), still he
was conscious of a distinguished air, and nodded
to the donkey to look at him.

While these were gazing at one another,
with free interchange of opinion, the rector of
the parish, on his little pony, turned the corner
bluntly. He was on his way home, at the
bottom of the coombe, not in the very best
temper perhaps, in spite of the sport in prospect; because Sir Roland had met so unkindly
his kind desire to know things.

"What have you got on your lap, boy?"
Mr. Hales so strongly shouted, that sulky Echo
pricked her ears; and "on your lap, boy," went
all up the lonely coombe melodiously.

Bonny knew well what was on his lap—a
cleverly plaited hare-wire. Bottler had shown
him how to do it, and now he was practising
diligently, under the auspices of his first hat.
Mr. Hales was a "beak," of course; and the
aquiline beak of the neighbourhood. Bonny had
the honour of his acquaintance, in that fierce
aspect, and in no other. The little boy knew

that there was a church, and that great people
went there once a-week, for still greater people
to blow them up. But this only made him the
more uneasy, to clap his bright eyes on the
parson.

"Hold there! whoa!" called the Rev.
Struan, as Bonny for his life began to cut away;
"boy, I want to talk to you."

Bonny was by no means touched with this
very fine benevolence. Taking, perhaps, a low
view of duty, he made the ground hot, to
escape what we now call the "sacerdotal office."
But Struan Hales (unlike our parsons) knew
how to manage the laity. He clapped himself
and his pony, in no time, between Master
Bonny and his hole, and then in calm dignity
called a halt, with his riding-whip ready at his
button-hole.

"It is—it is—it is!" cried Bonny, coming
back with his head on his chest, and meaning
(in the idiom of the land) that now he was
beaten, and would hold parley.

"To be sure, it is!" the rector answered,
keeping a good balance on his pony, and well
pleased with his own tactics. He might have
chased Bonny for an hour in vain, through
the furze, and heather, and blackberries; but

here he had him at his mercy quite, through his knowledge of human nature. To put it coarsely—as the rector did in his mental process haply—the bigger thief anybody is, the more sacred to him is his property. Not that Bonny was a thief at all; still, that was how Mr. Hales looked at it. In the flurry of conscience, the boy forgot that a camel might go through the eye of a needle, with less exertion · than the parish incumbent must use to get into the Bonny-castle.

"Oh hoo, oh hoo, oh hoo!" howled Bonny, having no faith in clerical honour, and foreseeing the sack of his palace, and home.

"Give me that wire," said Mr. Hales, in a voice from the depth of his waistcoat. "Now, my boy, would you like to be a good boy?"

"No, sir; no, sir; oh no, plaize, sir! Jack nor me couldn't bear it, sir."

"Why not, my boy? It is such a fine thing. Your face shows that you are a sharp boy. Why do you go on living in a hole, and poaching, and picking, and stealing?"

"Plaize, sir, I never steals nothin', without it is somethin' as don't belong to me."

"That may be. But why should you steal even that? Shall I go in, and steal your things now?"

"Oh hoo, oh hoo, oh hoo! Plaize, sir, I
han't got nothin' for 'e to steal."

"I am not at all sure of that," said the
rector, looking at the hermit's hole longingly;
"a thief's den is often as good as the bank.
Now, who taught you how to make this snare?
I thought I knew them all pretty well; but this
wire has a dodge quite new to me. Who
taught you, you young scamp, this moment?"

"Plaize sir, I can't tell 'e, sir. Nobody
taught me, as I knows on."

"You young liar, you couldn't teach yourself. What you mean is, that you don't choose
to tell me. Know, I must, and know I will, if
I have to thresh it out of you." He had seized
him now by his gorgeous waistcoat, and held
the strong horsewhip over his back. "Now,
will you tell, or will you not?"

"I 'ont, I 'ont. If 'e kills me, I 'ont," the
boy cried, wriggling vainly, and with great
tears of anticipation rolling down his sunburnt
cheeks.

The parson admired the pluck of the boy,
knowing his own great strength of course, and
feeling that if he began to smite, the swing of
his arm would increase his own wrath, and
carry him perhaps beyond reason. Therefore

he offered him one chance more. "Will you tell, sir, or will you not?"

"I 'ont tell; that I 'ont," screamed Bonny; and at the word the lash descended. But only once, for the smiter in a moment was made aware of a dusty rush, a sharp roar of wrath, and great teeth flashing under mighty jaws. And perhaps he would never have walked again if he had not most suddenly wheeled his pony, and just escaped a tremendous snap, well aimed at his comely and gaitered calf.

"Ods bods!" cried the parson, as he saw the jackass (with a stretched-out neck, and crest erect, eyes flashing fire, and a lashing tail, and, worst of all terrors, those cavernous jaws) gathering legs for a second charge, like an Attic trireme, Phormio's own, backing water for the diecplus.

"May I be dashed," the rector shouted, "if I deal any more with such animals! If I had only got my hunting-crop; but, kuk, kuk, kuk, pony! Quick, for God's sake! Off with you!"

With a whack of full power on the pony's flanks, away went he at full gallop; while Jack tossed his white nose with high disdain, and then started at a round trot in pursuit, to scatter them more disgracefully, and after them sent a fine flourish of trumpets, to the grand old national air of hee-haw.

While the Rev. Struan Hales was thus in sore discomfiture fleeing away as hard as his pony could be made to go, and casting uneasy glances over one shoulder at his pursuer, behold, he almost rode over a traveller footing it lightly round a corner of the lane!

"Why, Uncle Struan!" exclaimed the latter; "is the dragon of St. Leonard's after you? Or is this the usual style of riding of the beneficed clergy?"

"Hilary, my dear boy," answered the rector; "who would have thought of seeing you? You are come just in time to defend your uncle from a ravenous beast of prey. I was going home to bait a badger, but I have had a pretty good bait myself. Ah, you pagan, you may well be ashamed of yourself, to attack your clergyman!"

For Jack, perceiving the reinforcement, and eyeing the stout stick which Hilary bore, prudently turned on his tail and departed, well satisfied with his exploit.

"Why, Hilary, what has brought you

home ?" asked his uncle, when a few words had passed concerning Jack's behaviour. " Nobody expects you, that I know of. Your father is a mysterious man ; but Alice would have been sure to tell me. Moreover, you must have walked all the way from the stage, by the look of your buckles ; or perhaps from Brighton even."

"No; I took the short cut over the hills, and across by way of Beeding. Nobody expects me, as you say. I am come on important business."

"And, of course, I am not to know what it is. For mystery, and for keeping secrets, there never was such a family."

"As if you did not belong to it, uncle!' Hilary answered, good naturedly. "I never heard of any secrets that I can remember."

"And good reason too," replied the rector; "they would not long have been secrets, my boy, after they came to your ears, I doubt."

" Then let me establish my reputation by keeping my own, at any rate. But, after all, it is no secret, uncle. Only, my father ought to know it first."

"Alas, you rogue, you rogue ! Something about money, no doubt. You used to condescend to come to me when you were at school and college. But now, you are too grand for the purse of any poor Sussex rector. I could put off our badger for half-an-hour, if you think you could run down the hill again. I should like you particularly to see young Fox; it will be something grand, my boy. He is the best pup I ever had in all my life."

"I know him, uncle; I know what he is. I chose him first out of the litter, you know. But you must not think of waiting for me. If I come down the hill again, it will only be about eight o'clock for an hour's rabbit-shooting."

Since he first met Mabel Lovejoy, Hilary had been changing much, and in every way, for the better. Her gentleness, and soft regard, and simple love of living things (at a time when cruelty was the rule, and kindness the rare exception), together with her knowledge of a great deal more than he had ever noticed in the world around, made him feel, in his present vein of tender absence from her, as if he never could bear to see the baiting of any badger. Therefore he went on his way to his father, pitying all things that were tormented.

CHAPTER XXIV.

SIR ROLAND LORRAINE, in his little book-room, after that long talk with his mother, had fallen back into the chair of reflection, now growing more and more dear to him. He hoped for at least a good hour of peace to think of things, and to compare them with affairs that he had read of. It was all a trifle, of course, and not to be seriously dwelt upon. No man could have less belief in star, or comet, or even sun, as glancing out of their proper sphere, or orbit, at the dust of earth. No man smiled more disdainfully at the hornbooks of seers and astrologers; and no man kept his own firm doubtings to himself more carefully.

And yet he was touched, as nobody now would be in a case of that sort, perhaps, by the real grandeur of that old man in devoting himself (according to his lights) to the stars that might come after him. Of these the brightest now broke in ; and the dreamer's peace was done for.

What man has not his own queer little turns ? Sir Roland knew quite well the step at the door — for Hilary's walk was beyond mistake ; yet what did he do but spread hands on his forehead, and to the utmost of all his ability—sleep?

Hilary looked at his male parent with affectionate sagacity. He had some little doubts about his being asleep, or at any rate, quite so heartily as so good a man had a right to repose. Therefore, instead of withdrawing, he spoke.

"My dear father, I hope you are well. I am sorry to disturb you, but—how do you do, sir ; how do you do ? "

The schoolboy's rude answer to this kind inquiry—" None the better for seeing you "— passed through Hilary's mind, at least, if it did not enter his father's. However, they saluted each other as warmly as can be expected reasonably of a British father and a British son ; and then they gazed at one another, as if it was the first time either had enjoyed that privilege.

"Hilary, I think you are grown," Sir Roland said, to break the silence, and save his lips from the curve of a yawn. "It is time for you to give up growing."

"I gave it up, sir, two years ago; if the standard measures of the realm are correct. But perhaps you refer to something better than material increase. If so, sir, I am pleased that you think so."

"Of course you are," his father answered; "you would have grown out of yourself, to have grown out of pleasant self-complacency. How did you leave Mr. Malahide? Very well? Ah, I am glad to hear it. The law is the healthiest of professions; and that your countenance vouches. But such a colour requires food after fifty miles of travelling. We shall not dine for an hour and a half. Ring the bell, and I will order something while you go and see your grandmother."

"No, thank you, sir. If you can spare the time, I should like to have a little talk with you. It is that which has brought me down from London in this rather unceremonious way."

"Spare me apologies, Hilary, because I am so used to this. It is a great pleasure to see you, of course, especially when you look so well. Quite as if there was no such thing as money—which happens to you continually, and is your panacea for moneyed cares. But would not the usual form have done—a large sheet of paper (with tenpence to pay), and, 'My dear father, I have no ready cash—your dutiful son, H. L.' ? "

" No, my dear father," said Hilary, laughing in recognition of his favourite form; " it is a much more important affair this time. Money, of course, I have none; but still, I look upon that as nothing. You cannot say I ever show any doubt as to your liberality."

" You are quite right. I have never complained of such diffidence on your part. But what is this matter far more important than money in your estimate ? "

" Well, I scarcely seem to know," said Hilary, gathering all his courage, " whether there is in all the world a thing so important as money."

" That is quite a new view for you to take. You have thrown all your money right and left. May I hope that this view will be lasting ? "

" Yes, I think, sir, that you may. I am about to do a thing which will make money very scarce with me."

"I can think of nothing," his father answered, with a little impatience at his prologues, "which can make money any scarcer than it always is with you. I know that you are honourable, and that you scorn low vices. When that has been said of you, Hilary, there is very little more to say."

"There might have been something more to say, my dear father, but for you. You have treated me always as a gentleman treats a younger gentleman dependant upon him—and no more. You have exchanged (as you are doing now) little snap-shots with me, as if I were a sharpshooter, and upon a level with you. I am not upon a level with you. And if it is kind, it is not fair play."

Sir Roland looked at him with great surprise. This was not like Hilary. Hilary, perhaps, had never been under fatherly control as he ought to be ; but still, he had taken things easily as yet, and held himself shy of conflict.

" I scarcely understand you, Hilary," Sir Roland answered, quietly. " If you have any grievance, surely there will be time to discuss it calmly, during the long vacation, which you are now beginning so early."

" I fear, sir, that I shall not have the

pleasure of spending my long vacation here. I have done a thing which I am not sure that you will at all approve of."

"That is to say, you are quite sure that I shall disapprove of it."

"No, my dear father; I hope not quite so bad as that, at any rate. I shall be quite resigned to leave you to think of it at your leisure. It is simply this — I have made up my mind, if I can obtain your consent, to get married."

"Indeed," exclaimed the father, with a smile of some contempt. "I will not say that I am surprised; for nothing you do surprises me. But who has inspired this new whim, and how long will it endure?"

"All my life!" the youth replied, with fervour and some irritation; for his father alone of living beings knew how to irritate him. "All my life, sir, as sure as I live! Can you never believe that I am in earnest?"

"She must be a true enchantress so to have improved your character! May I venture to ask who she is?"

"To be sure, sir. She lives in Kent, and her name is Mabel Lovejoy, the daughter of Mr. Martin Lovejoy."

"Lovejoy! A Danish name, I believe; and an old one, in its proper form. What is Mr. Martin Lovejoy by profession, or otherwise?"

"By profession he is a very worthy and long-established grower."

"A grower! I fail to remember that branch of the liberal professions."

"A grower, sir, is a gentleman who grows the fruits of the earth, for the good of others."

"What we should call a 'spade husbandman,' perhaps. A healthful and classic industry—under the towers of Œbalia. I beg to be excused all further discussion; as I never use strong language. Perhaps you will go and enlist your grandmother's sympathy with this loyal attachment to the daughter of the grower."

"But, sir, if you will only allow me——"

"Of course; if I would only allow you to describe her virtues—but that is just what I have not the smallest intention of allowing. Let the wings of imagination spread themselves in a more favourable direction. This interview must close on my part with a suggestive (but perhaps self-evident) proposition. Hilary, the door is open."

CHAPTER XXV.

THE WELL OF THE SIBYL.

In the village of West Lorraine, which lies at
the foot of the South Down ridge, there lived
at this moment, and had lived for three generations of common people, an extraordinary old
woman of the name of Nanny Stilgoe. She
may have been mentioned before, because it
was next to impossible to keep out of her,
whenever anybody whosoever wanted to speak
of the neighbourhood. For miles and miles
around, she was acknowledged to know everything; and the only complaint about her was
concerning her humility. She would not pretend to be a witch; while everybody felt that
she ought to be, and most people were sure
that she was one.

Alice Lorraine was well-accustomed to have
many talks with Nanny; listening to her queer
old sayings, and with young eyes gazing at the

wisdom or folly of the bygone days. Nanny, of
course, was pleased with this; still she was too
old to make a favourite now of any one.
People going slowly upward towards a better
region, have a vested interest still in earth, but
in mankind a mere shifting remainder.

Therefore all the grace of Alice and her
clever ways and sweetness, and even half a
pound of tea and an ounce and a half of tobacco,
could not tempt old Nanny Stilgoe to say what
was not inside of her. Everybody made her
much more positive in everything (according as
the months went on, and she knew less and less
what became of them) by calling upon her, at
every new moon, to declare to them something
or other. It was not in her nature to pretend
to deceive anybody, and she found it harder,
from day to day, to be right in all their trifles.

But her best exertions were always forthcoming on behalf of Coombe Lorraine, both as
containing the most conspicuous people of the
neighbourhood, and also because in her early
days she had been a trusty servant under Lady
Valeria. Old Nanny's age had become by this
time almost an unknown quantity, several years
being placed to her credit (as is almost always
done), to which she was not entitled. But, at

any rate, she looked back upon her former
mistress, Lady Valeria, as comparatively a
chicken, and felt some contempt for her judgment, because it could not have grown ripe as
yet. Therefore the venerable Mrs. Stilgoe
(proclaimed by the public voice as having long
since completed her century), cannot have been
much under ninety in the year of grace 1811.

Being of a rather stiff and decided—not to
say crabbed—turn of mind, this old woman
kept a small cottage to herself at the bend of
the road beyond the blacksmith's, close to the
well of St. Hagydor. This cottage was not
only free of rent, but her own for the term of
her natural life, by deed of gift from Sir Roger
Lorraine, in gratitude for a brave thing she had
done when Roland was a baby. Having received this desirable cottage, and finding it
followed by no others, she naturally felt that
she had not been treated altogether well by the
family. And her pension of three half-crowns
a-week, and her Sunday dinner in a basin, made
an old woman of her before her time, and only
set people talking.

In spite of all this, Nanny was full of good-
will to the family, forgiving them all their
kindness to her, and even her own dependence

upon them ; foretelling their troubles plentifully,
and never failing to dwell upon them.   And
now on the very day after young Hilary's conflict with his father, she had the good luck to
meet Alice Lorraine, on her way to the rectory,
to consult Uncle Struan, or beg him to intercede.
For the young man had taken his father at his
word, concluding that the door, not only of the
room, but also of the house, was open for him,
on the inhospitable side ; and, casting off his
native dust from his gaiters; he had taken the
evening stage to London, after a talk with his
favourite Alice.

Old Nanny Stilgoe had just been out to
gather a few sticks to boil her kettle, and was
hobbling home with the fagot in one hand, and
in the other a stout staff chosen from it, which
she had taken to help 'her along.   She wore no
bonnet or cap on her head, but an old red
kerchief tied round it, from which a scanty iron-
grey lock escaped, and fluttered now and then
across the rugged features and haggard cheeks.
Her eyes, though sunken, were bright and keen,
and few girls in the parish could thread a fine
needle as quickly as she could.   But extreme
old age was shown in the countless seams and
puckers of her face, in the knobby protuberance

where bones met, and, above all, in the dull wan
surface of skin whence the life was retiring.

· " Now, Nanny, I hope you are well to-day,"
Alice said, kindly, though by no means eager to
hold discourse with her just now; "you are
working hard, I see, as usual."

" Ay, ay, working hard, the same as us all
be born to, and goes out of the world with the
sweat of our brow.   Not the likes of you, Miss
Alice.   All the world be made to fit you, the
same as a pudding do to a basin."

" Now, Nanny, you ought to know better
than that.   There is nobody born to such luck,
and to keep it.   Shall I carry your fagot for
you ?   How cleverly you do tie them ! "

" 'Ee may carr the fagot as far as 'ee wool.
'Ee wunt goo very far, I count.   The skin of
thee isn't thick enow.   There, set 'un down now
beside of the well.   What be all this news about
Haylery ? "

" News about Hilary, Nanny Stilgoe ! Why,
who has told you anything ? "

" There's many a thing as comes to my
knowledge without no need of telling.   He
have broken with his father, haven't he ?   Ho,
ho, ho ? "

" Nanny, you never should talk like that.

As if you thought it a very fine thing, after all you have had to do with us!"

"And all I owes you! Oh yes, yes; no need to be bringing it to my mind, when I gets it in a basin every Sunday."

"Now, Mrs. Stilgoe, you must remember that it was your own wish to have it so. You complained that the gravy was gone into grease, and did we expect you to have a great fire, and you came up and chose a brown basin yourself, and the cloth it was to be tied in; and you said that then you would be satisfied."

"Well, well, you know it all by heart. I never pays heed to them little things. I leaves all of that for the great folk. Howsever, I have a good right to be told what doth not consarn no strangers."

"You said that you knew it all without telling! The story, however, is too true this time. But I hope it may be for a short time only."

"All along of a chield of a girl—warn't it all along of that? Boys thinks they be sugar-plums always, till they knows 'en better."

"Why, Nanny, now, how rude you are! What am I but a child of a girl? Much better, I hope, than a sugar-plum."

"Don't tell me! Now, you see the water in that well. Clear and bright, and not so deep as this here stick of mine is."

"Beautifully cool and sparkling even after the long hot weather. How I wish we had such a well on the hill! What a comfort it must be to you!"

"Holy water, they calls it, don't em? Holy water, tino! But it do well enough to boil the kittle, when there be no frogs in it. My father told me that his grandfather, or one of his forebears afore him, seed this well in the middle of a great roaring torrent, ten feet over top of this here top step. It came all the way from your hill, he said. It fetched more water than Adur river; and the track of it can be followed now."

"I have heard of it," answered Alice, with a little shiver of superstition; "I have always longed to know more about it."

"The less you knows of it the better for 'ee. Pray to the Lord every night, young woman, that you may never see it."

"Oh, that is all superstition, Nanny. I should like to see it particularly. I never could understand how it came; though it seems to be clear that it does come. It has only come twice in five hundred years, according to what they say of it.   I have heard the old rhyme about it ever—oh, ever since I can remember."

"So have I heered.   But they never gets things right now; they be so careless.   How have you heered of it, Miss Alice?"

"Like this—as near as I can remember:—

'When the Woeburn brake the plain,
Ill it boded for Lorraine.
When the Woeburn came again,
Death and dearth it brought Lorraine.
If it ever floweth more,
Reign of the Lorraines is o'er.'

Did I say it right now, Nanny?"

"Yes child, near enough, leastways.   But you haven't said the last verse at all.

'Only this can save Lorraine,
One must plunge to rescue twain.'"

"Why, I never heard those two lines, Nanny?"

"Like enough.   They never cares to finish anything nowadays.   But that there verse belongeth to it, as certain as any of the Psalms is.   I've heered my father say it scores of times, and he had it from his grandfather.   Sit you down on the stone, child, a minute, while I go in and start the fire up.   Scarcely a bit of wood fit to burn round any of the hedges now, they

thieving children goes everywhere.   Makes my
poor back stiff, it doth, to get enow to boil a
cow's foot or a rind of bakkon."

Old Nanny had her own good reasons for
not wanting Alice in her cottage just then.
Because she was going to have for dinner a
rind of bacon truly, but also as companion
thereto a nice young rabbit with onion sauce ; a
rabbit fee-simple whereof was legally vested in
Sir Roland Lorraine.   But Bottler, the pigman,
took seizin thereof, *vi et armis*, and conveyed it
habendum, coquendum, et vorandum, to Mrs.
Nanny Stilgoe, in payment for a pig-charm.

Meanwhile, Alice thought sadly over the
many uncomfortable legends concerning her
ancient and dwindled race.   The first outbreak
of the "Woeburn," in the time of Edward the
Third, A.D. 1349, was said to have brought forth
deadly poison from the hillside whence it sprang.
It ran for seven months, according to the story
to be found in one of their earliest records, con-
firmed by an inscription in the church ; and the
Earl of Lorraine and his seven children died of
the "black death" within that time.   Only a
posthumous son was left, to carry on the lineage.
The fatal water then subsided for a hundred
and eleven years ; when it broke forth suddenly .

in greater volume, and ran for three months only. ' But in that short time the fortune of the family fell from its loftiest to its lowest; and never thenceforth was it restored to the ancient eminence and wealth. On Towton field, in as bloody a battle as ever was fought in England, the Lorraines, though accustomed to driving snow, perished like a snowdrift. The bill of attainder, passed with hot speed by a slavish Parliament, took away family rank and lands, and left the last of them an outcast, with the block prepared for him.

Nanny having set that coney boiling, and carefully latched the door, hobbled at her best pace back to Alice, and resumed her subject.

"Holy water! Oh, ho, ho! Holy to old Nick, I reckon; and that be why her boileth over so. Three wells there be in a row, you know, Miss, all from that same spring I count; the well in Parson's garden, and this, and the uppest one, under the foot of your hill, above where that gypsy boy harboureth. That be where the Woeburn breaketh ground."

"You mean where the moss, and the cotton-grass is. But you can scarcely call it a well there now."

' "It dothn't run much, very like; and I ha'n't

been up that way for a year or more.   But only
you try to walk over it, child ; and you'd walk
into your grave, I hold.   The time is nigh up
for it to come out, according to what they tells
of it."

"Very well, Nanny, let it come out.   What
a treat it would be this hot summer !   The
Adur is almost dry, and the shepherd-pits
everywhere are empty."

"Then you pay no heed, child, what is to
come of it, if it ever comes out again.   Worse
than ever comed afore to such a lot as
you be."

"I cannot well see how it could be worse
than death, and dearth, and slaughter, Nanny."

"Now, that shows how young girls will talk,
without any thought of anything.   To us poor
folk it be wise and right to put life afore anything, according to natur'; and arter that, the
things as must go inside of us.   There let me
think, let me think a bit.   I forgets things now ;
but I know there be some'at as you great folks
count more than life, and victuals, and natur',
and everythin'.   But I forgets the word you
uses for it."

"Honour, Nanny, I suppose you mean—the
honour, of course, of the family."

" May be, some'at of that sort, as you builds up your mind upon. Well, that be running into danger now, if the old words has any truth in 'em."

" Nonsense, Nanny, I'll not listen to you. Which of us is likely to disgrace. our name, pray ? I am tired of all these nursery stories. Good-bye, Mrs. Stilgoe."

" It'll not be you, at any rate," the old woman muttered wrathfully, as Alice with sparkling eyes, and a quick firm step, set off for the rectory : " if ever there was a proud piece of goods—even my bacco her'll never think of in her tantrums now ! Ah, well ! ah, well ! We lives, and we learns to hold our tongues in the end, no doubt." The old lady's judgment of the world was a little too harsh in this case, however ; for Alice Lorraine, on her homeward way, left the usual shilling's-worth of tobacco on old Nanny's window-sill.

CHAPTER XXVI.

AN OPPORTUNE ENVOY.

"It is worse than useless to talk any more," Sir Roland said to Mr. Hales, who by entreaty of Alice had come to dine there that day, and to soften things : "Struan, you know that I have not one atom of obstinacy about me. I often doubt what is right, and wonder at people who are so positive. In this case there is no room for doubt. Were you pleased with your badger yesterday ? "

"A capital brock, a most wonderfnl brock ! His teeth were like a rat-trap. Fox, however, was too much for him. The dear little dog, how he did go in ! I gave the ten guineas to my three girls. Good girls, thoroughly good girls all. They never fall in love with anybody. And when have they had a new dress—although they are getting now quite old enough ? "

"I never notice those things much," Sir Roland (who had given them many dresses) answered, most inhumanly; "but they always look very good and pretty. Struan, let us drink their healths, and happy wedlock to them."

The Rector looked at Sir Roland with a surprise of geniality. His custom was always to help himself; while his host enjoyed by proxy. This went against his fine feelings sadly. Still it was better to have to help himself, than be unhelped altogether.

"But about that young fellow," Mr. Hales continued, after the toast had been duly honoured; "it is possible to be too hard, you know."

"That sentiment is not new to me. Struan, you like a capeling with your port."

"Better than any olive always. And now there are no olives to be had. Wars everywhere, wars universal! The powers of hell gat hold of me. Antichrist in triumph roaring! Bloodshed weltering everywhere! And I am too old myself; and I have no son to—to fight for Old England."

"A melancholy thought, but you were always pugnacious, Struan."

"Now, Roland, Roland, you know me better.

' To seek peace and to ensue it,' is my text and
my tactic everywhere. And with them that
be of one household, what saith St. Paul the
apostle in his Epistle to the Ephesians ? You
think that I know no theology, Roland, because
I can sit a horse and shoot ? "

" Nay, nay, Struan, be not thus hurt by
imaginary lesions. The great range of your
powers is well known to me, as it is to every
one. Particularly to that boy whom you shot
in the hedge last season."

"No more of that, an' you love me. I believe
the little rascal peppered himself to get a guinea
out of me.   But as to Hilary, will you allow me
to say a few words without any offence ?   I am
his own mother's brother, as you seem very
often to forget, and I cannot bear to see a fine
young fellow condemned and turned out of
house and home, for what any young fellow is
sure to do.   Boys are sure to go falling in love
until their whiskers are fully grown.   And the
very way to turn fools into heroes (in their own
opinion) is to be violent with them."

" Perhaps those truths are not new to me.
But I was not violent—I never am."

" At any rate you were harsh and stern.
And who are you to find fault with him ?   I

care not if I offend you, Roland, until your
better sense returns.   But did you marry exactly in your own rank of life, yourself?"

"I married a lady, Struan Hales—your
sister—unless I am misinformed."

"To be sure, to be sure!   I know well
enough what you mean by that; though you
have the most infernal way of keeping your
temper, and hinting things.   What you mean is
that I am making little of my own sister's
. memory, by saying that she was not your
equal."

"I meant nothing of the sort.   How very
hot your temper is!   I showed my respect for
your family, Struan, and simply implied that it
was not graceful, at any rate, on your part——"

"Graceful be hanged!   Sir Roland, I cannot express myself as you can—and perhaps I
ought to thank God for that—but none the less
for all that, I know when I am in the right.   I
feel when I am in the right, sir, and I snap my
fingers at every one."

"That is right.   You have an unequalled
power of explosion in your thumb-joint—I
heard it through three oaken doors the last
time you were at all in a passion; and now it
will go through a wall at least.   Nature has

granted you this power to exhibit your contempt of wrong."

"Roland, I have no power at all. I do not pretend to be clever at words ; and I know that you laugh at my preaching. I am but a peg in a hole I know, compared with all your learning; though my churchwarden, Gates, won't hear of it. What did he say last Sunday ?"

"Something very good, of course. Help yourself, Struan, and out with it."

"Well, it was nothing very wonderful. And as he holds under you, Sir Roland——"

"I will not turn him out, for even the most brilliant flash of his bramble-hook."

"You never turn anybody out. I wish to goodness you would sometimes. You don't care about your rents. But I do care about my tithes."

"This is deeply disappointing, after the wit you were laden with. What was the epigram of Churchwarden Gates ? "

"Never you mind. That will keep—like some of your own mysteries. You want to know everything and tell nothing; as the old fox did in the fable."

"It is an ancient aphorism," Sir Roland answered, gently, " that knowledge is tenfold better than speech. Let us endeavour to know things, Struan, and to satisfy ourselves with knowledge."

"Yes, yes, let us know things, Roland. But you never want us to know anything. That is just the point, you see. Now, as sure as I hold this glass in my hand, you will grieve for what you are doing."

"I am doing nothing, Struan; only wondering at your excitement."

"Doing nothing! · Do you call it nothing to drive your only son from your doors, and to exasperate your brother-in-law until he blames the Lord for being the incumbent instead of a curate, to swear more freely? There, there! I will say no more. None but my own people ever seem to know what is inside of me. No more wine, Sir Roland, thank you. Not so much as a single drop more! I will go, while there is good light down the hill."

"You will do nothing of the kind, Struan Hales," his host replied, in that clear voice which is so certain to have its own clear way; "you will sit down and take another glass of port, and talk with me in a friendly manner."

"Well, well, anything to please you. You are marvellous hard to please of late."

"You will find me most easy to please, if only (without any further reproaches, or hinting at things which cannot concern you) you will favour me with your calm opinion in this foolish affair of poor Hilary."

"The whole thing is one. You so limit me," said the parson, delighted to give advice, but loath to be too cheap with it; "you must perceive, Roland, that all this matter is bound up, so to speak, altogether. You shake your head? Well, then, let us suppose that poor Hilary stands on his own floor only. Every tub on its own bottom. Then what I should do about him would be this: I would not write him a single line, but let him abide in his breaches or breeches—whichever the true version is—and there he will soon have no halfpence to rattle, and therefore must grow penitent. Meanwhile I should send into Kent an envoy, a man of penetration, to see what manner of people it is that he is so taken up with. And according to his report I should act. And thus we might very soon break it off; without any action for damages. You know what those blessed attorneys are."

Sir Roland thought for a little while; and then he answered pleasantly.

"Struan, your advice is good. I had thought of that course before you came. The stupid boy soon will be brought to reason; because he is frightened of credit now; he was so singed at Oxford. And I can trust him to do nothing dishonourable, or cold-blooded. But the difficulty of the whole plan is this. Whom have I that I can trust to go into Kent, and give a fair report about this mercenary grower, and his crafty daughter?"

"Could you trust me, Roland?"

"Of course I could. But, Struan, you never would do such a thing?"

"Why not? I should like to know, why not? I could get to the place in two days' time; and the change would do me a world of good. You laity never can understand what it is to be a parson. A deacon would come for a guinea, and take my Sunday morning duty, and the congregation for the afternoon would rejoice to be disappointed. And when I come back they will dwell on my words, because the other man will have preached so much worse. Times are hard with me, Roland, just now. If I go, will you pay the piper?"

"Not only that, Struan; but I shall thank you to the uttermost stretch of gratitude."

" There will be no gratitude on either side. I am bound to look after my nephew's affairs : and I sadly want to get away from home. I have heard that there is a nice trout stream there. If Hilary, who knows all he knows from me, could catch a fine fish, as Alice told me,—what am I likely to do, after panting up in this red-hot chalk so long ? Roland, I must have a pipe, though you hate it. I let you sneeze ; and you must let me blow."

" Well, Struan, you can do what you like, for this once. This is so very kind of you."

" I believe if you had let that boy Hilary smoke," said the Rector, warming unto his pipe, " you never would have had all this bother with him about this trumpery love-affair. Cupid hates tobacco."

END OF VOL. I.

www.ingramcontent.com/pod-product-compliance
Lightning Source LLC
Chambersburg PA
CBHW060555030726
47498CB00005B/1394